Beauty & The BEARD

R.M. NEILL

Contents

Dad, this one was for you.
I wish you could have seen it.
"Why be miserable? It doesn't accomplish a damn thing."
I miss you.
1947-2023

Author's Note

Please be aware grief for a lost spouse is a prevalent theme in this story. There's also off-page past emotional and sexual abuse. Should any of these topics be sensitive to you, please protect yourself and don't continue reading.

Chapter 1
Sasha

"You're actually going to live in the wilderness for a month? What if a bear eats you?"

"Then it might get indigestion. A bear isn't going to fucking eat me, Roman. Honestly."

Shaking my head at my friend's rather uninformed comment, I stuff more wool socks into my suitcase. I know I won't get eaten by a bear, but I heard wool socks are good for hikes. I hope to do a lot of those. Commune with nature and all that shit.

"What are you going to do there for a whole month? There are no theatres or malls or anything. Like... won't you get bored?"

Roman's tone suggests his boredom would hit in about seven minutes if he were at my wilderness retreat.

"Well, the whole point is to try to unplug a little and just... think about my life. Read books. Stay away from people. Watch sunsets and stuff. Maybe eat some marshmallows over the fire."

"Oh, I love those! With the chocolate and little wafer things?"

A real smile lifts my lips for the first time in what feels like years. I flop on the bed next to my best friend, Roman, and prop up my head with my hand.

"Yeah, the gooey chocolate and marshmallow stuff between graham crackers. Sticky fingers and smell like a campfire."

"And bug spray." He wrinkles his nose. "Don't forget bug spray. I read about that stuff. It's nasty." His smile drops. "It could stain clothes, Sasha."

"Well, it's necessary for where I'm going. But they have showers, Roman. I won't be dropped in the middle of the wilderness left to fend for myself. Here, look." Pulling the brochure off my nightstand, I hand it to Roman. "This is where I'm going. There's a pretty lake and a town fifteen minutes away. I have a suite in this lodge building here."

Tapping the photo, he glances sideways at me.

"Sasha, it's like... old."

"It's rustic and charming, Ro. And it's where I want to be. My friend Heath booked it all for me. I trust him."

Mostly, I trust him. But since he helped me during a tough time, I like to give back. He needed some experience in vacation planning, so I gave him a list and this is what he came up with. As long as there's some kind of internet connection, I'll be fine. Yes, I want to step away from the drama of my life for the past eighteen months, but I need to stay connected. Surely he wouldn't send me somewhere without the internet.

"Besides, Ro, I need to do something. Think of it as a retreat of sorts. I need to find myself and consider my next moves now. I'm no longer part of Fresh Faces Modelling. I need to figure out my life."

Which is the biggest understatement ever. My current life looks like the aftermath of a tornado. Soon, the court case, lawsuits, and the upcoming sentencing will finally close the door on that part of my life. While I've been trying to right myself and move ahead, the constant spotlight has made it more difficult. My mental health has nosedived. For my sanity, I need to just get away.

"He did you dirty, Sasha. Moe's judgement is coming and he'll get what he deserves. I know you took the biggest hit by coming forward, but others will step up now. I know it."

Swallowing the lump in my throat, I stare at the ceiling of my small studio apartment. After I take this much needed downtime, I'll be back to pack up and move on from the only life I've ever really known. And, hopefully, start over.

Roman rolls over again, smacking the brochure back on my chest.

"Okay, seriously, what if you encounter a bear?"

"Depending on the type, I might throw myself at him." I waggle my eyebrows and Roman at least chuckles at my joke.

"I know you're teasing me and maybe I sound ridiculous, but I really am worried about wildlife there. You're a city boy, Sasha. I know you're fierce, but did you know bears can run up to thirty-five miles per hour?"

"Uh, no."

"And sometimes they stalk people. It's rare, but it happens."

"I had no concerns about bears until we had this conversation. Thanks, Ro."

"Just stay safe, okay? I know you don't always like to take instruction," he holds up his hand to stop my protest. "But please listen to them. I want my friend back intact and not fished out of the belly of a hungry bear."

"God, Roman. Have you been watching *Wild Discovery* again?"

He pushes off the bed and heads towards the door.

"They had a marathon last week. It was interesting."

Roman grabs his coat off the rack by my door and turns to me, his arms open for a hug. I step into my friend's embrace with a smile.

"I promise I'll be back—in one piece—before you know it."

"I love you, Sash. Let me know once you're there safe."

"I will as soon as I can. I love you, too."

I kiss his cheek, and he squeezes me back before leaving with a wave.

After the door clicks behind Roman, I turn my deadbolt. A quick glance at the clock confirms I don't have that much time left to finish packing and get to the airport.

But even knowing I'm on a time crunch, I have to google black bears.

Then I gasp.

Damn Roman and his wildlife shows.

The flight was smooth and my town car pick up at the airport was very comfortable. I used the two-hour car ride to text Roman that I'd landed safely and slug back the *Starbucks* latte I snagged in the airport before my ride arrived to take me on the next leg of my journey.

We drove out of the city of Montreal, through farmland and gorgeous backdrops any painter would flock to for inspiration. Vineyards rolled past and my excitement grew. There was already so much to see and explore and I hadn't even arrived at the lodge yet.

My driver pulled into a very run-down service station and parked. He sent a text on his phone before turning back to me.

"This is where I leave you to your next driver. I'll grab your luggage."

Following the driver out of the car, I scan the lot for another town car. Perhaps there's a limit on how far he can take a fare and he needs to pass me off to another company.

"Will the wait be long?" I ask, since the only other vehicle in the parking lot is a rusty old *Toyota Corolla* and a giant yellow school bus.

My driver cocks his head, like maybe I'd missed a very important piece of information.

"You're going to Maple Mountain Lodge, right?"

"That's right."

He hefts my luggage and walks towards the bus. The bus door swings open with a squeak and he passes my bags to someone inside.

"This bus takes you the rest of the way."

Sweat breaks on my brow. Confession: I've never been on a bus - not for school or even public transit. School buses are creepy and city buses are full of... just *ick*. And don't even get me started on subways. Mass public transportation is not for me.

"Uh, how much farther is it?"

A grey-haired man pokes his head out from the bus and motions me to come inside.

"You must be Solomon Montpellier." He extends a hand when I'm within range. "The name is Pete, and I'll be taking you the rest of the way."

Taking his hand, I shake it, perhaps with a grip of more fear than welcome.

"Please call me Sasha. Nobody calls me Solomon."

His warm smile calms me as he motions to the back of the bus.

"Sure thing, Sasha. Pick a seat and we'll get rolling. It's thirty minutes up a country side road to the lodge. The fancy cars don't like to drive it. That's why we have a bus."

The bus rumbles to life and I'm thankful to be the only passenger. I take the first seat in the front, and clutch the cracked green pleather seat edge when the bus lurches out of the parking lot. Pete secured my luggage in a rack on one side of the bus, and when I steal a quick peek around, I notice most of the seats have been removed.

"So, Pete," I raise my voice over the impossibly loud rumble of the yellow beast. "How come you use a bus for this? Are there usually more guests for you to pick up on each trip?"

"Usually. You're arriving on a Wednesday. Most people arrive and leave on Fridays and Saturdays." He shifts down to navigate the bus onto the side road. There's a community mailbox at the corner with a billboard smothered in flyers. A rural version of the office water cooler.

"And the seats we take out because most people travel here with a lot of gear. Like fishing or hunting equipment. And if they take home animals, they need space."

"Animals?"

The bus wheels hit a pothole and we shimmy and shake. My fingers dig further into the bus seat. Do these things tip over?

"Yeah, like moose or partridge or fish. Used to be bear, but most of our guests tend to be fishermen these days. Or photographers. Or people like yourself who just want to be with nature for a while."

Oh god. What have I allowed Heath to get me into?

"Oh."

Dust swirls into the open windows as we travel up the road. It's muggy in the bus with no air conditioning and the seats are as hard as a park bench in winter. Anxiety about this being the right step for me seeps in. Maybe I should have booked a beach vacation instead.

A few pickup trucks roar past us, dust plumes in their wake, so it's not that secluded if people actually live up this road. That's a small comfort. Even if my mind is still stuck on the possibility of bears.

Finally, the bus pulls into a wide entrance, and a gorgeous lake comes into view. It's smooth as glass, surrounded by forest as far as I can see. The reflection of the trees gives the water a green shade that reminds me of a synthetic emerald ring my mom used to have. Pete leads the bus in a circle style drive and we come to a halt in front of the main lodge.

Rustic is what us city folk use to refer to decor at the *Pottery Barn* and *Pier One*. Anything with wood tones and fake birch bark. It's cute.

This is not rustic or what I'd call a '*wilderness paradise*', according to the pamphlet.

It's not even a little utopian.

The lodge is an enormous log cabin. Pete opens the bus doors and I step out while he grabs my luggage. The lodge has a porch running along the front with rough timber. Not the lumber you find in the home improvement stores, but lumber that looks... homemade? Cut by hand anyway.

The windows are clean and new-ish, not quite married to the lodge look, but I suppose you need windows to be functional and it was the best fit.

A man wearing a fishing vest and hat with several lures stuck to it exits while I stare. He smiles and nods and, in his garish black rubber boots, he walks to the dock at the lake's edge. A small boat is tied to the end and I stare, completely fascinated as he starts the motor, pushes off the dock, and putters off. All by himself.

"I'll carry your bags inside and we'll find out where Leaf has you booked in."

Leaf.

"Is Leaf the manager of the place?"

He grunts what I assume is an affirmative and huffs up the stairs with a suitcase. I open the door for him and when I step inside... well, I'm pleasantly surprised.

The lodge isn't filled with trophies of stuffed animal heads or fish. It does, however, have photos of what I assume are people who came here and were successful, showing off their fish and animals. But it's light and airy, welcoming and with a strong vibe of found family for whoever happens to stay here. Perhaps it's the gingham-checked window toppers or the giant *'Enter as guests but leave as Friends'* sign, but whatever it is feels like a huge hug.

It's also filled with the heavenly aroma of sugar. Maple sugar.

Pete leads me to a little alcove with a sign that says main office. The sign is hand written on a piece of wood and while obviously homemade, it just suits the place.

"Leaf! You in here?"

"Don't bellow at me, old man. I heard you rattle up, and I was coming."

The deep, gravelly voice belongs to a giant of a man, not dressed in hunt clothes or anything woodsy really, but a pair of faded blue jeans, a too tight hunter-green Henley and an apron that says, *I lick spoons.*

His ebony hair is just beginning to show flecks of grey that are more noticeable in his beard. And even though his voice is intimidating, his eyes aren't. Not for Pete, anyway. They twinkle and smile as he gives Pete a quick hug before turning to give me a once over.

I clutch my *Kenneth Cole* messenger bag closer and lower my eyes. You'd think I'd be used to the stares of hungry men, but no matter who they are, it always makes me uncomfortable. Living your life in the spotlight is fabulous for developing self-esteem issues. And I have plenty.

"You must be Mr. Montpellier. Your friend booked you for a month. What is it you've come here to do for a month?"

While he speaks he's flipped open a reservation book and made a note. Behind him is an honest to god key rack, and he plucks one off. A giant wooden maple leaf is attached to the key with the words, 'Cabin Number Three' on it.

Lord, the quaint charm about a paper reservation book and an old fashion door key warms my soul. Sure, I wasn't overly impressed by the exterior a few moments ago, but since stepping inside, it's hard to resist the comforting pull of the place.

"Uh, I just needed out of the city. Explore nature. That sort of thing."

Again, his gaze roams over me, and I don't know if it's good or bad.

"Pete will show you to your cabin. I hope you don't mind not being in the main building. Your friend said you were looking for quiet, so I gave you the best place I have."

My cheeks warm under his gaze with the knowledge he gave me the best room here. Hospitality so far is a five-star rating.

"Thank you. I'm sure I'll be fine."

"You'll find the meal service times in your room. Dinner tonight starts at 5 P.M. Just show up before 6 P.M. and you'll get fed. If you have any questions, I'm always around."

I take the proffered key from his hand, and he waves a goodbye to us.

Pete smiles and hefts my bag back up.

"You'll love Cabin Three."

Back outside we go, and I make sure to take one of my smaller bags at least. Pete chatters as we walk down a path to a hidden beach and I gasp.

"This is beautiful."

A sandy beach lies ahead with three small cabins tucked at the edge of the forest. Each little cabin has its own tiny porch with a hammock on a stand. Firepits are set up on the beach and there are solar light poles scattered along the path. I bet that will be pretty at night time.

Hopping up the steps to Cabin Three, I turn the key, and a new thrill courses through me. I've never stayed in a cabin before. It's not much bigger than my apartment, but I fall in love with it immediately. The cabin is one giant room with a bathroom at the back. After dropping my bags at the door by Pete, I rush to the ladder leading up to a loft.

"Is the bedroom up here?"

My voice squeaks and Pete nods.

"You can sleep up there if you'd like or on this thing here." He walks over to a box that I thought was a closet and turns the latch. With a tug, a bed slides out and settles on the floor.

"This is the coolest thing ever!"

I can't decide if I want to roll on the secret bed from the wall or climb up into the loft made for cool kids.

"I'll let you get settled, but be sure you get over to the lodge for dinner. If you want food for the cabin while you're here, Leaf can arrange it for you. He's always up at the main building if you need anything."

"Thank you so much, Pete. And I'm sorry if maybe I came off as a snob earlier. It's been an overwhelming day. A lot of new things have happened for me and sometimes I don't know how to respond."

"No apologies needed." He assesses me and I feel like he might want to say something, but stops himself. "Just be sure to ask Leaf for anything. He loves a good customer experience. It's important to him for you to enjoy yourself."

"I will. Thank you again."

With a wave, Pete leaves, closing the door behind him.

And I close my eyes to rest on the softest, most comfortable bed out of a wall and promptly fall asleep.

Chapter 2
Leaf

"Are you going to go check on him? I don't think he's used to this kind of getaway. He might need some guidance."

Millie wraps a plate of leftovers and places it in the fridge with a pointed look in my direction.

"I know that look, Millie. Pete said he was excited about the cabin and seemed fine."

My lodge cook and mother figure wags a finger at me.

"Leaf Albert Attwater." Stepping closer, she cranes her neck back to peer up into my face. At six-foot-two, I tower over her diminutive five-foot even, but she's the only person here that can intimidate me. "Don't hide from him. I know your heart might still hurt, but that boy is broken. I can tell."

"Mother's intuition?"

She hums. "Something like that."

"Is this you telling me *he* needs someone or you telling me *I* need someone?"

Her face softens, and she takes my hand.

"No one can ever fill the space Connor left, sweetie. I understand that. But I don't want you to waste away here. There's a whole world for you to see. More life in you to live."

I know she's right. I've been trying, but it feels like every time I consider possibilities, my heart cries to stay where it's safe.

"I know, Millie. It's just… I don't know. Maybe that window closed. I'm forty-three years old and the dating scene isn't the same as it was twenty years ago. I can't just leave here."

She returns to cleaning up the evening meal service and I glance at the clock. It's after 7 P.M. and there's still no sign of the pretty man with the haunted eyes. He'll be hungry. Opening the fridge, I remove the plate Millie made for him and cradle it like a live grenade.

Millie pauses her duties when I still don't move from the fridge.

"It's okay, Leaf. Connor wouldn't expect you to grieve for him forever. You're just bringing a guest his dinner. Talk to him. Maybe you'll be friends and maybe not."

Her gentle voice soothes the guilt that comes up every time I think of meeting someone new.

"He's probably hungry. I'll bring this and go check on him."

She squeezes my arm. "Wonderful idea. He shouldn't miss my pan-fried pickerel, anyway. I bet he'll appreciate the welcome. He's very city, isn't he?"

Laughing, I smile back at her. "You noticed, huh?"

"Well, it wasn't hard. The matching *Louis Vuitton* luggage kinda gave it away. Most people here have pack sacks and duffle bags when they arrive." She chuckles again. "And they don't show up in designer clothes unless it's *North Face* or *Columbia*. He'll need some help, Leaf."

She's right. My initial reaction was to ask him what he was trying to prove, showing up clearly not dressed for anything at a mountain lodge. I thought maybe he was flaunting his wealth at first, but the way he avoided my gaze and seemed to squirm in my presence said that wasn't it. Millie noticed the same thing I did. Something was not quite right with my out-of-place, yet very attractive guest.

The least I could do was bring him the dinner he missed.

"Okay, I'm on my way over. I'll see you tomorrow."

Leaning down, I drop a kiss to the top of her head and head out to Cabin Three. It's a gorgeous evening in June. The moon shines across the lake's surface and throws an ethereal glow onto the path to the cabins.

This was always one of my favourite places to walk at night. It had the best view of the moon's glow across the water and it always felt like a spotlight was shining, waiting for some great story to unfold in the blanket of darkness.

When I reach Cabin Three, there are no lights on inside. What if he really is asleep and doesn't want to be disturbed? But he has no food in there either. I can't in good conscience have him out here without a morsel to eat. If Connor were here, he'd rip me a new one for not caring about a guest's well-being.

With a deep breath, I knock lightly on the door. A few moments pass and I hear no movement. My heart races with fear and worse case scenarios, but I talk myself down. Not everything ends in disaster, Leaf. He's likely just a heavy sleeper.

Knocking louder this time, I wait and there's a crash inside.

"Sasha! Are you in there?"

What feels like forever passes until he opens the door a crack. Sleep creases from his pillow line his face, and his hair, once perfectly styled, is all smashed on one side.

"Leaf! Oh thank god! I thought you were a bear, and I didn't know what to do."

Stifling a laugh, I hold up the plate.

"Well, bears won't knock on the door. And I brought you dinner. You missed the evening meal."

He blinks at the plate and back at me and I'm not sure what I see in his eyes. It's not distrust. There's something else.

"Oh, I'm so sorry. How do I... uh... is there a microwave here?" He runs a hand over his face. "I didn't even look around once Pete left. I just laid down and instantly crashed."

"Can I come in? I'll show you around the place and what to do."

He opens the door for me to step through and I reach for the light switch. The kitchen light flickers and comes to life. Sasha's luggage still stands by the door and I step around them.

"Travelling is always tiring, isn't it? Where are you from?"

Pushing back the nerves of making conversation with an attractive man, I toe off my shoes and walk to the kitchen.

"Uh, I came here from a town called Rosevale, but I'm originally from a small town in Northern Ontario where there are more mosquitos than people. I moved away when I was just a child, though, so I barely remember it."

Nodding, I smile as I open the cupboard for a frying pan. At least he knows about mosquitoes. That's a good thing.

"There's no microwave here. But you have a full set of cookware and the stove is propane. You just have to turn the knob here for it to light. It's like an indoor bbq."

Setting the pan on the element, I locate the cooking spray in the cupboard with the staples we provide and coat the pan before dumping the plate of food in.

"I've never had a BBQ."

Sasha creeps closer now and watches as I stir around the food and his belly grumbles loud enough for me to hear. When I laugh, his cheeks flush pink.

"Sorry. I really am starving. Thank you for doing this for me. But..." He trails off and I wait with a ball of dread. I never asked if he had a food allergy. "I don't mean to sound rude, but part of the reason I came here was to learn to be more self-sufficient. I want to do things for myself."

There's no malice in his words. He's simply being upfront and telling me why he's here. There's definitely no reason for me to bristle over it. And yet I still do.

Stepping away from the stove, I motion for him to take over and, after hesitating, he picks up the wooden spoon and gingerly stirs the food around.

"It smells wonderful. What kind of fish is this?"

He inhales deeply over the pan and, for a moment, I lose myself to the memory of serving Connor fish for the first time. But Connor is gone and this pretty waif of a thing now waits expectantly for my answer. None the wiser of my inner reflection.

"It's pickerel. Caught in the lake on the weekend. I only serve it when there aren't a lot of guests here." He raises a well-manicured eyebrow in question. "You can only catch so many at once," I explain. "Since I'm only one person, I catch my limit for a few days, then feed it when there's a smaller group."

"That makes sense." He chews his lip before darting a glance my way. "How do I know when it's ready?"

Instinctively, I reach for the spoon but draw back, remembering his earlier words.

"You can use the spoon and take a piece of potato out of the pan to the countertop. Test it with a bite. If it's warm enough, the rest should be as well."

Nodding and eager, he plops a piece of potato on the counter. He opens the drawer, locating the cutlery on the first try, and nabs a fork. Once he brings the piece to his mouth, his eyes twinkle with a joy I've only seen once before, and after touching it to his lips with a small laugh, he puts it in his mouth and chews.

"*Ohmygod*! It's so good."

"If it's warm enough, take down a plate and just dump it all on there. You're ready to eat."

He does just that and sets the pan back down on the element. As he turns to take the food to the table, I grab his arm.

"You need to turn the element off first. If you leave it on with a pan like that, you might burn the place down."

A small gasp exits his lips and he turns to study the stove knobs. Brow furrowed, my heart goes out to him because he's unsure. Has he really never used a stove top?

"The little diagrams next to the dial tell you what element it's for." Reaching in front of him, I click the button to off and the tiny poof of the flame extinguishing sounds.

"Thank you. You probably think I'm a loser. Not knowing how to work a stove."

Pulling out a chair at the table, I seat myself, and he joins me. The embarrassed flush to his cheeks only makes him more attractive. Bedhead and all.

"Well, we all need to learn sometime. Maybe you've only used a microwave or cooked over fires. I don't know."

He says nothing, but I'm happy he's eating the food. Millie's fish is simple, but so damn good. It'd be a shame if he couldn't experience it.

"Would you teach me how to fish?"

Startled by the question, I cock my head.

"Is that what you'd like?"

"Maybe?"

We both laugh as he cleans his plate and once again I'm drawn to his eyes. There's a lot of emotions swimming there. Things I can't quite pull out, but I wonder why such a city guy felt like he needed to flee to the middle of nowhere in Québec to cope with it.

Or maybe I'm just reading too much into this whole thing and he really is just a guy looking to broaden his horizons.

"If you want to learn how to fish, now is the perfect time. There's a spot across the lake where the bass are biting. They're a lot of fun to catch and I guarantee you'll catch something."

He smiles so sweetly I want to lie down and let him do whatever he wants with my body. And this is very new for me. My heart pounds with a forgotten rhythm that both excites and frightens me.

"Yeah? So I could actually catch a real, honest-to-god fish? By myself?"

Sasha's eyes shine. His excitement at such a foreign possibility zings in the air and I can't help but share the feeling with him.

"Well, first you need to define what you mean by *yourself*. Are you only reeling it in, or will you bait the hook, too?"

I thought he'd balk at the bait question, but he considers it as he fidgets with his fork.

"All of it. I want to bait the hook, reel it in... but, and I'm sorry if this is silly..." he chews his lip. "Can we let it go?"

"Of course we can. Lots of people like to fish for fun, Sasha. They catch a fish, take a picture, and throw it back."

I jolt when he hoots a laugh and pushes his chair back.

"Can we go tomorrow?"

"I'll have to check what's on my schedule first. I might make it happen."

"Shit. I'm sorry. You run this place and here I am asking you to be my personal tour guide. You probably have a lot of better things to do than cater to a spoiled city guy who doesn't even know how to use a stove."

"Actually, it would be my pleasure and while I do run the place, I have people I trust to fill in. I don't get to fish as much as I'd like, and taking you out would be wonderful." His eyes widen and it's my turn to feel the heat on my neck. "Taking you to fish, I mean. Not on a date."

Nodding, he takes his plate over to the sink and another foreign feeling creeps in. The need to stay and talk for hours. To find out everything about him, from his toothpaste brand to if he likes to eat popcorn at a movie. The need to have a companion again—in *all* the ways I can.

Overwhelmed, I push my chair back and head to the door.

"Have a good night, Sasha. Breakfast is at 7 A.M.. I'll speak to you then about fishing."

Without another word, I hotfoot it back to the lodge and up to my suite. My private apartment is away from the guest rooms and sits at the back of the lodge overlooking the lake. Once inside, I slump against the door with a sob.

"How can I let someone else in after you, Connor? I don't know how to let you go."

The silence in the room allows my words to hang in the air like the morning mist on the lake. Again, there's no answer to the question I've been asking myself for seven years.

Alone, I slide into bed and stare at the ceiling until my eyes finally grow heavy with sleep, yet my heart beats with the hope that I might have an answer to my question soon.

Chapter 3
Sasha

"How is it possible to not have a single bar of cell service here?"

After a fitful sleep filled with thoughts of the handsome lumberjack owner of this place, I thought I'd research what's involved with fishing. It might be a good idea to not appear like a complete moron and throw some slang around. Or at least understand the proper terminology.

With no internet or cell service, I woke up early and unpacked instead. I read the welcome manual in the cottage and learned I need to get my own food for the cabin if I didn't want to join them for meals in the lodge. The town is nearby and it wouldn't hurt to stock up on snacks just in case. I'm not sure if I'm confident enough to cook on the stove without Leaf here, but prepackaged food sounds like a great idea. If Leaf can't take me fishing today, I'll inquire how to get to town and maybe even explore a little once I get there.

But really, how come my phone can't get service? It worked at the gas station when Pete picked me up. Looking up things about fishing isn't the only thing I need internet for. I really want to talk to Roman about Leaf.

When I first arrived, he was intimidating, but not in a power trip way. He was a man in control. He was confident. He was also breathtakingly handsome. I could tell he had a sharp, cut jaw-even under his short beard-and his deep brown eyes shone with both a sadness and a profound longing. In his faded jeans and tight Henley, he was the picture of every woodsman fantasy. All he needed was a plaid shirt and an axe.

But I kept my usual flirt game under wraps. Here I wasn't Sasha the former model and people pleaser. I was just Sasha. A man trying to use the quiet of nature to think about life and find my purpose. Just a man trying to figure out how to blend in so that I could start over.

And my plan didn't include the loss of cell service and the internet. Nobody told me the woods were an internet-free zone. Sure, I said I wanted to unplug, but not completely.

With that thought in mind, I exit my cabin and walk the short path up to the lodge. The haunting call of a bird, a loon I'm pretty sure, carries across the water and I stop to listen. When I do, I notice it's not all I hear. A faint rustle of leaves in the intermittent breeze, the gentle lap of water on the shore, and the loon.

There are no sirens or horns honking. No drunk people shouting and no music competing to be heard over the horns and voices.

It's simple and quiet. The lack of barked orders in my direction and commands to turn this way, turn that way or get under the desk are silent. For the first time since I was forced into my life as a model, a blanket of ease settles over my soul. The only thing that would make this perfect is a coffee. Preferably a Starbucks café mocha, but I'll take whatever caffeine is in the lodge.

"It's a beautiful view, isn't it?"

Slapping a hand to my chest, I whirl and find Pete smiling at me.

"It's gorgeous. And you scared the hell out of me. I didn't hear you."

"Sorry. I move lightly so as not to startle any critters."

"What sort of critters?"

Dear god, have I unknowingly put myself in danger?

Pete chuckles, clearly knowing what's running through my mind.

"Rabbits mostly. Sometimes a fox. Nothing that will attack you or to be afraid of."

"Are there bears around?" I whisper, in case one is nearby, and decides to appear.

"Sometimes. Usually in the spring, they wander through and again in the fall. If we see them, we put up signs to advise people to just be aware."

"Isn't it still spring now?"

My peaceful morning has now switched to an itchy anxiety with the knowledge that sometimes bears come here. Now

I want to yell at Roman for planting this stupid fear in my head while simultaneously asking for information about the resident lumberjack.

Pete claps me on the back, steering me to the lodge.

"You're fine. Come on. You look like you could use some caffeine. How did you sleep last night?"

"After you left, I crashed until after 7 P.M.. Leaf brought dinner over to me since I missed it. I slept great, but I was awake far too early."

Pete glances at me as we climb the steps to the main lodge.

"Leaf brought you food to the cabin?"

"He did. And showed me how to use the stove. I've, uh, never used one like that before."

"We learn new things every day," Pete says easily and I'm relieved. "I'm glad he brought you food. Did you like the fish? Millie is an excellent cook."

Pete opens the door for us, and we enter the lodge, still chatting. There are only two other groups in the dining room, both are groups of four older men who raise their coffee cups to us when we enter.

A tiny woman in an apron stands next to one group, chatting, and when she sees us, she excuses herself and walks our way.

"You must be Sasha. I'm Millie. It's wonderful to meet you."

She offers her hand with a motherly smile and I instantly know I'll like her.

"Nice to meet you." I take her warm hand and even touching her like that makes me feel like I'm in the right place. "You cooked incredible fish last night. Best food I've had in a long time."

"Fancy city food has nothing on good home cooking. Maybe I'll teach you some before you go back."

Shocked, my mouth drops and I stammer a reply.

"I- I, um... a cooking lesson? I'd love that!"

"What will you love?"

The delicious, warm voice of Leaf pours over my body as he stops next to our group.

"I'm giving him a cooking lesson before he goes home."

Leaf's lips twitch and his gaze travels over me. "Seems like you'll get your wish and have a lot of new experiences before you go back to the city." He glances at the diners heading out for the day. "Did you have breakfast yet?"

"No. Pete found me on the way in. I was coming up but got lost in the beauty of the loon and the lake. It's really peaceful in the morning here."

Leaf nods, rather non-committal for the guy who hyped it up last night.

"Sasha, what would you like for breakfast?" Millie's hand on my arm draws a smile to my face. The gentle squeeze a comfort to the heartache I've long buried.

"Uh, whatever you tend to serve is fine. I don't want to be any trouble."

"Well, I wouldn't ask if it was trouble. Do you like pancakes?"

Licking my lips, I can't resist. "Big fluffy ones?"

Millie laughs at my excitement.

"The best kind. You can help yourself to a coffee over at the station, and I'll bring you a giant plate of pancakes."

She points to the coffee before bustling off to the kitchen. Swallowing, I face Leaf and Pete.

"Would you like to join me for coffee? I assume you both already ate."

Leaf nods, but gestures towards the coffee and follows behind me. Pete fills a take out cup and excuses himself, off to do whatever else it is he does here.

"It's no fancy city coffee. Just normal grocery store stuff, but sometimes Millie has flavoured creamer out."

Leaf keeps his head down as he speaks and I wish he'd look me in the eye. His tone is one I'm used to. The assumption that I'm a spoiled brat and not appreciative of life's small things. That I'm above the basic coffee he has to offer me.

"I just need caffeine. You could serve it in an old shoe and I'd drink it. I admit I love the fancy coffees, but I'm not a diva who might throw a fit because you only have full fat milk and no oat milk."

My tight reply has Leaf finally bringing his gaze to mine.

"I'm sorry. I didn't mean to imply–"

"It's fine. I'm used to the assumptions. But... let's start over."

Truth is, I'm more than used to it. I became them. At some point it was too much, too hard, to remain *me*. If someone expected the model to throw a fit over the lack of oat milk, I would. Sometimes it was easier than explaining I'm not a pretentious asshole just because I get paid to model underwear. Most times, it was easier than behaving how I wished I always could.

"Ah, so, do you still want to go fishing?"

Leaf takes a seat across from me at the table. A group of men carrying fishing rods and coolers enter the dining space, speaking animatedly about *the one that got away*. When they veer off to the main reception area, Leaf excuses himself.

"I need to see what they need. I'll... don't leave, okay?"

Nodding, I sip my coffee, but before he gets too far, I call after him.

"Leaf! Do you have any Wi-Fi access here?" He strides back to my table with a shy smile. "No, not yet. They just moved from dial-up here last year. But if you have a data plan, you get a decent signal here near the windows."

He leaves me again to tend to the guests and I'm left stuck on the fact they still had dial-up internet in this area until last year. No wonder he still keeps a paper reservation guest book.

My phone shows three bars of service here, near the window like Leaf said, and instead of trying to message on social media where he usually is, I text Roman instead.

Sasha: The internet connection sucks here. I can only text you from the lodge.

> I'm fine. My cabin is slick, and the owner
> is… nice. Very lumberjack. Easy on the
> eyes.

I don't really know how to describe Leaf by text. But he is nice. And tall. Very tall. Let's not forget ruggedly handsome in a way that makes me want to feign the injured ankle bit and see if he'd scoop me into his muscled arms.

Huh. That's not a bad idea.

"Here you are, sunshine."

Millie places a mammoth plate of pancakes in front me with what I can only describe as a vat of maple syrup in a giant metal gravy boat.

"Are you feeding an army? That's a lot of pancakes." Inhaling over the fluffy pile of goodness, saliva rushes into my mouth. "They smell heavenly. Oh my god, please don't let me eat this entire plate."

It's like Christmas. Or what I imagine a proper Christmas would be.

"I wasn't sure what your appetite would be like. I didn't want you to be hungry. Especially if you plan to be fishing with Leaf today."

Pouring the maple syrup over the pancakes, I watch as the fluffy pieces suck it all in and become so saturated with syrup they lose a bit of fluffiness.

"He didn't confirm we were going today." I stuff a giant forkful into my mouth and moan. "This is amazing. What makes this taste like nirvana, Millie? Can you teach me to make these?"

"Oh, he didn't tell you? He arranged for Perry, his brother who guides for us, to cover around here in case I need help. I've packed you both lunches, and he's taking you fishing after breakfast."

"Really!?"

She nods with a giant smile as I keep shovelling the maple-soaked goodness into my yap. I don't know if it's the maple syrup or the pancake, or the combo together, but I can't get enough of it.

"This syrup tastes better than any other syrup I've ever had. I just realized this is what I smelled when I first arrived. Maple syrup or maple sugar."

"Thank you." Leaf joins us again and sips from his now-cold coffee. "I made that batch last year. It's one of my best."

My fork clatters on the plate, and I stare at Leaf. Lips parted and thoughts swirling all over like confetti in the wind.

"You make maple syrup? For real?"

Could this man be any more god-like? He creates sugar. It's my most favourite food group next to chocolate.

Millie laughs softly and Leaf's lips tick up in a shy smile.

"Is that what it takes to impress you? Make maple syrup?"

"You already impressed me. The syrup is just... well, it's an addition to the list of desirable features."

Millie pats my arm. "Enjoy your day, sunshine. I'm glad you like the pancakes. I'll see you later."

"I could show you how," Leaf blurts and quickly looks away. "But you tap the trees early. It's a February or March thing. When there's still snow. Most people don't come here much then. But I mean, that's when sap happens. For the syrup."

He clears his throat and stares into his cup. It was an adorable ramble about... well, I'm not quite sure, but I know it means something for him to say it.

"I'd consider it. Being here with snow, I mean."

He puffs a small breath before gracing me with a real smile.

"Uh, good. You might change your mind after fishing. If you still want to go, that is."

Pushing my empty plate aside, I'm shocked I finished the entire stack of pancakes.

"I wouldn't have asked if I didn't want to go."

Leaf shifts in his chair and stares back into his coffee cup. His body language is hard for me to read, but I'm positive Leaf is just as careful around people as I am.

"Okay." He finally nods, committed to the idea. "Millie made us lunch. Perry is on his way and I already made sure the boat was ready to go this morning. You can change and we'll head out."

"Change?"

I dressed very conservatively today in my white linen pants, loafers, and a loose fitting t-shirt in a gorgeous pastel blue. It's the softest material and perfect for a day on the lake. Or at least I thought so.

"Um… do you have jeans? A long sleeve shirt and shoes you don't mind if they get wet? Clothes that might get dirty?"

My phone chooses that moment to buzz with a text and we both glance at it. Right there for Leaf to see is the response from my best friend, Roman.

Roman: A hot lumberjack! Do tell!

Mortified doesn't begin to describe how I feel, but I flip the phone over with a grace I didn't know I possessed.

Clearing my throat, I meet Leaf's curious gaze.

"I have jeans, but I'm afraid I just brought t-shirts. And hiking boots. And a gorgeous pair of *Michael Kors* sandals."

"I don't know who Michael Kors is, but I'll take your word for it. Even a pair of running shoes is fine. I'll get you a long sleeve shirt to borrow." He pushes out of his chair. "I'll meet you back here in twenty minutes. Is that enough time?"

"Yep. I can do that."

He nods, and before he walks away, he gestures to my phone with a knowing smile.

"Tell your friend I'm not a real lumberjack. I just look like one."

Closing my eyes and drowning with embarrassment I wait until he's gone before answering Roman's text.

Sasha: He saw this text! I'm going to die of embarrassment!

> **Roman:** Or get plundered by a lumberjack! Oh, wait. That's a pirate thing. Anyway, so he's cute? You've been there one day and you're already crushing.

Taking a chance, I dart out the lodge doors and check my service. I still have a three-bar signal, so I hit Roman's contact and duck behind the corner of the lodge. The docks are down the grassy slope to the lake, and the view is just as beautiful as it was this morning.

"Sasha, is everything ok? I was only kidding about the plundering! Sort of."

"It's easier than texting, and I'm fine. I only get limited reception here, but listen, I need to be fast. Last night he brought supper to my cabin and showed me how to use a propane stove. We talked, and he's nice. And he says he only looks like a lumberjack, by the way. But he was super hesitant about things. Like, I'm pretty sure he's interested, but he's not a rushing kind of guy."

"And he's not actually a lumberjack. That's disappointing."

"Ugh. I can't believe he saw that text. And it's not disappointing, believe me. Listen, I need to change and he's taking me fishing."

"Like for fish?"

"What else do you fish for?"

"I don't know. Compliments? Squid? A way into your pants?"

Annoyed with my friend not picking up on how huge this is, I decide to just move on.

"Ro, he's handsome. Supremely so and... he treated me like an equal. Even when I couldn't figure out the stove. I like him based on his looks alone and if he wanted to have a fling while I'm here, I'd be open to it. But this is about me, remember? I didn't come here looking for love. I'm looking for peace."

"Sorry, Sasha. You're right. I'm super proud of you. Are you sure you'll be able to handle fishing? That's different even for you. It's way beyond a ride on a mechanical bull."

"I know. But I'll let you know how it goes. I need to go. Just don't worry if you can't reach me. The cell and internet service here sucks."

"Probably because they don't want you on your cell phones when you have so many other things to do there. Good luck and wear a life jacket!"

Shaking my head at Roman, I tell him I will before saying goodbye and hotfoot it back to my cabin. Once inside, I decide the low sweatpants with running shoes I wore on the plane and a fitted t-shirt are the most fishing acceptable attire I have, and quickly change.

And Roman is right. Why do I need a phone when there's so much more to do here?

Instead, I grab my camera bag and head back up to the lodge, actually excited about the possibility of catching a fish.

Chapter 4
Leaf

How should I feel knowing the cute man in Cabin Three told his friend I'm a hot lumberjack?

My guess is I shouldn't be feeling like I just caught the flu bug and need to hurl.

"I better bring *Rolaids* on the boat, just in case."

With a shirt for Sasha and a few Rolaids in my pocket, I head out of my suite and stop in the kitchen for our lunch.

Millie greets me with a knowing smile and doesn't even let me protest the hug she gives. But as always, she knows I need the anchor of her affection and I return the gesture.

"You're excited this morning, Leaf. Are you okay?"

"I think I'm nervous. He's cute, right?"

She laughs before turning to the fridge.

"He's very cute. And he's also nice. He seems very surprised you're taking him out on the boat. Why do you think that is?"

Millie removes enough food from the fridge to feed twelve people and begins packing it into a cooler in the shape of a red-and-white bobber.

"I don't know, but he said he wants to learn how to do things himself. He wants experiences."

She hums under her breath. "You're a good man for that."

She nestles a bag of cookies on top of the food before closing the lid and I'm stuck on her words. I am a good man. I know that in my heart and nobody needs to reassure me of it. But should I do this?

"Millie, is this smart? He's technically a guest here. I own the place. I don't want to be unprofessional."

With her hands on her hips, she straightens her tiny frame, and still doesn't reach my shoulders.

"Don't give me that bullshit. Perry fucks anything that throws him a smile and you've not heard anyone complain, have you?"

Shocked Millie even knows about Perry's indiscretions, I stammer a response.

"N-no, but I'm the face of the lodge. It's a bit different."

She gathers a smaller cooler with drinks and ice before throwing her best mom look my way. The one that says, *are you really that clueless*?

"Leaf, nobody is forcing you to do anything here. You're the one who offered to take him fishing when you never go out with guests anymore. You brought him supper, and you enjoyed his company. You smiled a lot this morning, for heaven's sake. If he makes you happy, even just a tiny bit, chase it."

A flash of Connor catching his first fish runs through my mind and my heart bursts with the happy memory while breaking with the loss. I miss the days of laughing in the sun and kisses stolen in the cloak of darkness while the forest sleeps.

I'm not stuck in the past. I'm afraid of a future. One that might be better than the one Connor and I shared. It's hard to let go of the perfect feeling that was Connor and me taking on the world. Part of me is afraid to move forward and the other part of me begs to let go. To chase, like Millie says, and find another person should be something easy and free. But how do I do that when Connor is all I ever think about?

"You should go. He'll be here soon." She murmurs and hands me the coolers. "Leaf, enjoy the day with a man who may surprise you. If nothing comes of it, you've made a friend. Friends can never be too plentiful."

"Thanks Millie. I love you."

Dropping a kiss to her head, I exit the lodge just as Sasha appears from the trail and god, he's beautiful. Classic beauty that really belongs on the pages of a magazine. Full lips, sharp cheekbones, and eyes that sparkle like diamonds in the sun.

He's changed as I asked and while still not appropriate fishing wear, it's much better. Especially since it's my view for the day. Low hanging sweatpants that draw my gaze to the sliver of smooth skin peeking out between his shirt and waistband and stokes a fire in me that's been dead for a long time.

"Hi." He waves his hand comically, like a child, and grins. "I hope this is better for the boat? I thought I'd be more comfortable in sweatpants."

"You look great."

I probably shouldn't have complimented his appearance. But a small twitch of lips confirms it's not unwelcome.

He pauses and licks his lips. They're shiny with gloss, and I hope it at least contains SPF. I also love the look on him. Which is yet another thought I've not allowed myself to have since Connor. Appreciating the attractiveness of someone other than my dead husband sends waves of panic through me.

"Th-thank you."

Sasha grips the camera bag he's carrying closer and nibbles at his lip.

I feel like an awkward kid finally talking to his secret crush and I motion towards the dock.

"Well, let's get started then. Have you ever been on a boat?"

"Just a speedboat thingy for a photo shoot once. It had this huge bow with cushions and a bunch of us had to model *Speedos* and such. The boat never moved. They anchored us in a bay the whole time."

"Okay, so you're not familiar with boat safety then."

His brow furrows. "I wasn't then either."

The clipped tone of his voice raises the hair on my neck. But his sweet smile remains when he turns to me.

"I trust you, Leaf. I'm not sure why, but I don't think you'll steer me wrong."

"I'd never." I breathe.

Sasha nods to confirm my statement and marches alongside me to the dock. I cast a few sideways glances as we approach the boat, but he's as calm as a duck on the water. If he's nervous, I've yet to see any indication of it.

Arriving at the side of the boat, I instruct him to stay on the dock while I secure the coolers. I'd already loaded bait, rods and tackle, and checked the life jackets and safety gear earlier today. Holding my hand out to him, I instruct him to step into the front.

His soft hand, small and almost dainty, slides into my giant one and grips with shocking strength. He steps into the boat and, when it sways with his step, he holds tighter.

"Whoa. I should've been expecting it to sway." His laugh is both nervous and excited, and I smile back at him.

"You'll get your sea legs quick. Before we go, here's a long-sleeved shirt to wear. It's chilly when it's early and especially once we move on the water. Put that on and then your life jacket."

He sets the bag he's carrying on the seat and accepts the shirt I hand him. We both laugh once it's on. The sleeves pour past his hands and the hem hangs mid-thigh.

"I feel like a kid playing dress up."

Stepping forward, I roll up the sleeves on one side for him.

"Is that how you got into modeling? Playing in your parents' closet?"

The smile drops from his face and he gently pulls his arm from me. Rolling up the other sleeve himself, he shakes his head.

"No. It wasn't something I chose for myself."

His voice is barely a whisper and his chin wobbles.

"Hey, I'm sorry. I didn't mean to make you sad. I was just trying to get to know you a little."

He wipes a tear off his cheek and smiles again. The pain in his eyes is now as clear as the shallow water in the bay.

"It's okay, Leaf. I'll... maybe when we're fishing, I'll tell you. That's what you do when you fish, right? Talk about stuff while you wait for things to happen?"

"Or you smoke cigars and listen to the radio. Or silence. Depends on the day."

He cocks his head.

"Smoke cigars? You have some?"

Nodding, I grin. "It's a pleasure I save for boating. And I won't do it unless you're okay with it. Just because we're on the water doesn't mean it's a smoking zone. If you don't like it, just say so."

He shakes his head, smiling and excited once again.

"It's something else I've never tried." He grabs his life jacket, and I step forward to adjust the buckles. "Let's do this, Leaf. We'll catch fish and smoke cigars and shit."

Laughing harder than I have in years, I push us off the dock and head us out toward our destination at the end of the lake.

The boat ride to the bass spot I want to take Sasha to is a thirty-minute trip at full rip but instead of blasting us out there super fast, I slow down halfway so we can talk.

"Is that a camera bag you brought?"

"It is!" He smiles back as he pats the bag. "When I first started modelling, the camera equipment enthralled me. But some cameras were absolute monsters. I took a beginner class as an elective when I went to university and I've had this little baby ever since. It's a *Canon Rebel* and I've taken some stunning photos with it."

It's easy to notice how much more animated Sasha is over photography than talking about modelling. His enthusiasm is real.

"What did you take at university?"

"Oh," he chuckles, "I had high hopes of owning a business one day. I have a degree in economics and a certificate in small business planning."

"Wow. That's amazing. What kind of business did you want to start?"

He grows quiet again, and I think I've made another mistake in my conversational choice.

"Um, it's a long story, but I just wanted to be my own boss. Make my own decisions. That kind of thing. That's the reality of it. As for what kind of business it would be, it would still involve a camera." He fidgets with the cuffs of my too-long shirt and gazes at the shoreline. "What made you decide to own and run a lodge?"

My pulse races, and my tongue grows thick. I should have known he'd ask this question. It's a normal question. And it deserves an honest answer.

"I didn't decide. I inherited it. From my husband. He, uh, died seven years ago."

Swallowing hard, I stare straight ahead and brace for the pity that always comes when people learn I'm a young widower. It's not usually me that tells them, but one of the staff or Millie mentions it if asked.

Sasha shocks me, though. There's no pity. He's appreciative?

"What a wonderful gift. He must have loved you very much to leave this to you. I'm sorry you lost him, but you must feel close to him every day here. Was he a nature lover like you?"

The ease with which his questions and my answers come shocks me. I can't think of a time when it felt almost easy to speak about Connor.

"He was. His family owned this property for generations. Over the years, they built the lodge and then together we added the little cabins along the beach. He grew up here. He loved it."

"What was his name?"

Flicking my eyes to Sasha, I notice he's taken his camera out and points it at the shoreline.

"Connor. He was a nature nut. Then I came along and bought the sugar bush up the road. A city guy looking for an escape. He teased me relentlessly while I got started."

Connor definitely beat his way past my walls to capture my heart. I never intended to move here permanently and run a lodge with him. Never mind marry him. But I did, and they were some of the best years of my life.

"Did he tease you about being a citified lumberjack?"

Sasha laughs and points his camera at me.

"Well, I've always had a love of plaid and yes, he did. Because the first time we met, he saw me chopping wood with an axe and he made a remark about how the log drivers would have loved me in the bunkhouse." I smile with a small shake of my head. "Connor was *very* straightforward when he wanted something."

The sheltered cove I want to anchor at is up ahead and I motion for Sasha to look forward.

"We're going to anchor just off that rock face for the afternoon. You might get some great photos as the sun changes position."

Sasha shifts his focus and so do I. But not where it immediately should be. Since I've slowed the boat to a crawl as we enter the bay, he's walked to the front of the boat and knelt down. His sweatpants stretch over his hips and he's lost in taking photos. I don't want to disturb him from his zone, but I'm also caught up in it.

Because I was the same way when Connor introduced me to this life. I was so addicted to fishing after the first few times, I wondered if someone had drugged me.

A laugh sneaks out and Sasha peers over his shoulder at me. "What's so funny?"

"I was just remembering the first time I came fishing here and how quickly I was addicted. I'm wondering if the same will happen to you."

"There's only one way to find out!"

Christ. The smile and the laughing. The ease of speaking to him about Connor. The natural beauty of Sasha. It's been years since I've felt so comfortable and light.

And maybe I've missed moments like this more than I thought.

Killing the engine, I direct Sasha to sit while I anchor us. He snaps photos of everything the entire time.

I take out two fishing rods and show him how to use them. He casts and tries it out, all the while a giant smile on his face, like a five-year-old who got a second dessert after supper.

"Now comes the part most people hate. Bass love worms. You can put the worm on yourself or I can."

"So, it's alive and you just thread it on?"

He wrinkles his nose, and I take a worm from the container to show him. He watches, but he's not thrilled.

"You don't have to. I can do it for you."

"Would you? I think I need to work up to that part. Maybe the next time we come out, I can try."

The *next time* part isn't lost on me. His gaze meets mine and I know it was hard for him to ask me to bait his hook. Someone has hurt him. I know because it's the same tone my voice would carry when I finally asked for help myself. It never makes sense, but I worried if I asked for help with anything I'd be less. Less strong, less of a man, less than Connor deserved. Of course I know better now, but I'll never forget that feeling.

"That's absolutely fine with me." I put the worm on his hook and wipe my hands on a towel. "Now, how do I work this camera? You should have a picture of this."

"Oh god," he laughs but shows me how to point and shoot. "Roman will want to see this."

Effortlessly, he smiles and I point the camera at him. His pose isn't staged, and he's laughing. I press the button multiple times to capture the memory. In a moment of spontaneity, I hold up a finger. "Wait!"

Rummaging in the front pocket of my coat, I pull out my pack of colt cigars.

"Let this dangle from your lips. We'll get that full fisherman feel for Roman."

"Are you gonna light it?"

"When you catch your first fish, we will."

As I predicted, Sasha loves catching bass. Every tiny fish he reels up and fights to get in the boat, he laughs so big I swear I can see every tooth in his mouth. And if that wasn't enough to convince me he's enjoying himself, the constant giggles and shouts when his rod tip bounces with a bite is a sure sign I've just hooked him on fishing. I've lost track of how many fish he's caught now, but I could watch him all day.

"I don't think I've ever had this much fun." He plops into the chair and rubs a hand across his stomach. "But I'm starving. Can we eat?"

And that's how I let Sasha into my heart.

He enjoyed the water and the fish. He puffed on a cigar and I've laughed so hard my cheeks hurt. And now I'm setting up a table at the bow of the boat and unpacking the food Millie made for us.

Sasha is a breath of fresh air in a room with the windows painted shut. As he pops pieces of fruit in his mouth and clicks off more photos, I'm sad our time together today is nearing an end.

But I want more days with him before he leaves. More laughter. More of this feeling, that life can still be like this, even for only a short time.

"I have a full lodge booked next week for the start of summer vacation. I might not get to take you out fishing again until the following week. But I'd love to do this again with you."

"You have a business to run. It doesn't stop for me. I can amuse myself. In fact, I'd love to look at the photos we took today and print some. Is there a place in the town I could visit? Even a *Walmart* would be good."

"Um, I don't actually know, but after Pete gets the guests shuttled in, I can ask him to take you to town if you'd like. You can explore and see what's there. Ask around. There's a drugstore that might have a kiosk."

"You don't go into town much?"

Shaking my head, I spread some cream cheese on a cracker. "Not anymore. It was... uncomfortable after Connor died. I've kept to myself up here, mostly."

He nods, thoughtful, and chews more fruit.

"You know, I understand what you mean. Sort of. That's how I felt when I had to live with my guardian after Mom died. I didn't want to leave the house because everyone whispered about the new kid who was too pretty to be here. It was easier to hide in my room."

A silence falls on our conversation, but it's not unwelcome.

Because it seems like we have something in common.

A loss we don't like to talk about.

Chapter 5
Sasha

Back in my cabin after an amazing day with Leaf, I strip out of my clothes and step into the tiny shower. The scent of his *Colt Cigars* lingers in my hair and I'm sweaty from the warm day's sun. Perhaps even a little fishy. After all, I caught fish, and I even held one for a picture.

As the water flows over me, I close my eyes, and there's Leaf. Vivid behind my eyelids like the dream he is. Not since I met Roman at my first photo shoot, have I ever felt more comfortable with someone and able to be myself. He laughed with me and taught me things I never thought I'd ever do. All without expecting anything in return.

It's a refreshing change of pace not being pressured into something I don't feel comfortable with. Like the photo shoot on the boat I told Leaf about. If he knew that project turned into something with more skin than clothes for a private project against my protests, I don't think he'd be the calm, quiet guy he's been so far.

Done with my shower, I choose an outfit for dinner. Leaf asked me to hang around after supper tonight, and while I know it's not a date, I take extra time to apply some light makeup. Nothing too dramatic. I don't get any homophobic feels here, but you never know when you're dropped off in the middle of nowhere if they live in the current time or are still locked in the closet with their bibles.

Either way, Leaf appreciated my lip gloss earlier. I noticed him looking.

Keeping it simple, I focus on a bit of eyeliner and a pink-tinted lip gloss. Leaving my hair tousled, I rub a bit of mousse through it, and dress in a pair of khaki linen pants and a fitted red t-shirt.

With my camera bag and phone, I leave the cottage again and follow the path up to the lodge. It's still early before dinner starts and I want to explore more near the main building. Take some photos outside and walk more of the grounds.

My cottage had a map of the grounds and the trails nearby to hike. I'm not dressed for hiking, but there was something nearby I wanted to check out quickly before dinner.

Map in hand, I begin the walk up the road a few hundred meters and follow the flagged trees to a winding, single lane path. The tree leaves rustle in the breeze and squirrels trill constantly along with the buzz of mosquitos in my ears. It's a very morose roadway. A sorrow seems to hang in the air, and when I reach the end, a small cabin appears. It's clearly abandoned with grasses tall against the side and windows covered in dust. The larger building off to the right, though, that's what I'm here to see.

A sign above the door reads, *Leaf's Sweet Shack,* and my heart melts. What a cute name for his sugar shack. Of course, it's not time for syrup making as he explained to me, but I peer in the windows to see shelves of equipment, a giant wood stove and huge shiny metal vats that remind me of the brewery my friend Zane owns.

There's also a small building in front that appears to be the store he used to sell from. Grass and weeds surround it and the only building in recent use appears to be the Sweet Shack.

Snapping photos of it all and changing lenses, I take as many photos as I can before heading back for dinner. There's a feeling here that's off. It's hopeful and sad at once. While Leaf spoke of this place with happiness, I feel like it might also be too much for him to come here.

A motor sounds as I walk down the path and an ATV barrels down the lane towards me, stopping next to me with a dusty skid. Another giant of a man is driving and I wonder if they just grow them big here.

"Are you Sasha?"

"Uh, yes?"

"I'm Perry. I saw you heading this way earlier, and it didn't look like you were prepared for evening mosquitos. I thought I'd come and offer you a ride back to the lodge."

"I, ah, don't have a helmet, though."

Eyeing the machine he's driving, I'm not sure how I feel about riding in it. There're no doors or seatbelts and it's very,

very dusty. I may be here for new experiences, but also, I did my hair.

Perry smirks, pulls a blanket out of a bag at his feet, and lays it across the seat.

"You don't need a helmet for this. Don't mess your hair. Although Leaf might like seeing you in a helmet... just sayin'."

My heart thumps against my chest. Leaf would like me to wear a helmet? Should I?

"Uh, why is that?"

Perry grins and slaps the seat next to him.

"Get in. Because he's my brother and I know him well."

I do as he asks, and he holds out a helmet for me. It's black with orange flames up the side and it's kind of badass. I think I'd like to feel like a badass just once. After settling it on my head, I hand Perry my phone.

"Do you mind snapping a pic of me? My friend won't believe I did something like this."

He takes the photo, and when he passes the phone back, a laugh bubbles out of me.

"Okay, Perry. Punch it."

He booms a laugh so loud it almost drowns out the motor of the machine.

"Are you a *Star Wars* fan? I'm not *Chewbacca*. But I like it. Now hold on to your potatoes. It's not warp speed, but we'll go fast."

Gripping the handle above my head hard enough to turn my knuckles white, I nod. Perry spins the tires before swinging us in a circle and blasting back down the drive to the main road. It's fast. It's scary and I'm laughing and screaming like the world will end the entire time.

When he pulls up at the lodge, it's barely been a few minutes since I sat on the four wheeled machine, but I'm dusty and my cheeks hurt from laughing. Perry kills the engine and helps me unbuckle the helmet.

"There's a washroom just inside the lodge near the reception desk. You might want to pop in there and wash the dust from your face. Did you like the ride?"

"I'm not a fan of getting so dusty, but it was like an amusement park ride! So yes, I liked it."

"Great. I'll see you around. Maybe I'll take you out again if you want."

"Yeah! I'd love that, thanks!"

Perry takes off and I enter the lodge with possibly the biggest smile on my face in my life. I see the sign for the washroom and head to it, but stop when I hear Leaf's voice. He's in the reception room and it sounds like he's on the phone since I don't hear any other voices.

"I'm sorry. I just don't do the syrup like I used to. It's just a hobby for me and to supply the lodge. I wish I could help."

There's a long silence and I peek around the corner as Leaf turns and finds me in the door way.

"Thank you for the interest."

He replaces the phone back in the cradle and steps towards me.

His dark eyes are unreadable, and his hand reaches up to my face. A thumb wipes across my cheek and his lip twitches just a tiny bit into a smile.

"You have a lot of dirt on your face. It's cute."

"I, uh, was about to go wash up and I didn't mean to eavesdrop. I was..." I motion toward the washroom. "Perry told me to clean up over here."

Leaf's gaze roams over me and for the first time since meeting him, I'm very self conscious of my appearance. Wrapping my arms around myself, I glance towards the doorway and he notices.

"Hey, I didn't mean to make you uncomfortable." With a tentative hand, he reaches out and grazes his fingertips down my arm, and I shiver. "I just... you're... you look nice. I just wanted to tell you that."

"Thank you."

Our gazes meet and I'm overwhelmed. "I'm, ah, I'll clean up and see you at dinner?"

"I wouldn't miss it."

Nodding, at a loss for words for the first time ever, I turn and flee to the washroom. Once inside, I lean against the door and puff out a breath.

What the fuck just happened?

My shaking hands turn the faucet on, and I grab some paper towels. After wetting them and wringing them out, I wipe the dirt from my face and stare at the reflection looking back at me.

The helmet only flattened my hair a little and I run my fingers through it to puff it back up. My eye make-up is still on point, but there's a flush to my cheeks that wasn't there before. From the wind or the sun today, possibly, but I like it. It's not fake. A sign I lived today and did something to create a physical reminder.

And the memories that go with the photos are something I hope never fade.

"Sasha? You okay?"

A light tap on the door followed by Leaf's voice breaks me out of whatever dream land I drifted off to.

Opening the door, I peer up into concerned eyes.

"Sorry. I'm okay. I was just... I'm fine."

Again, he reaches out and gently squeezes my arm. It's tentative, like he's unsure how I'll respond. Or maybe even how he will. His chin trembles and he forces a smile on his lips.

"You didn't come out, and I was worried you... I just wanted to make sure you're okay."

The slight tremble in his voice has me rush to reassure him. Although I'm not sure why. But I do, and I step closer, placing a hand on his firm chest.

"I was only looking at myself in the mirror and noticing how different I looked after one full day here. Perspective, I guess."

His hand closes over mine with a gentle squeeze.

"And did you like what you see?"

Nodding, I swallow and meet his eyes.

"Very much." I whisper.

"Me too."

A moment passes. Two. And I can't tear my eyes away from this gentle giant with a broken heart and tender soul.

"Excuse me?"

Millie clears her throat, and Leaf drops my hand, spinning to address her.

"Yes?"

"Dinner is ready. If you want to help me bring it out to the buffet, I'd appreciate it."

"I'll be right there. Thanks, Millie."

With a nod and a smile in my direction, she returns to the kitchen.

"So, ah, I'll help Millie and I'll see you once everyone is eating?"

"Of course. I can help, too, if you'd like."

A genuine smile fills his face.

"You're a guest here. While I appreciate your offer, that's a no. Please sit and I'll join you after."

He flashes another smile before disappearing and I almost want to lock myself in the bathroom again, but a friendly voice stops me.

"Sasha. Care to join me?"

Perry has returned. No longer dressed in grubby overalls, he changed to jeans and a lodge branded t-shirt and ball cap. He has the same physique as his brother. Tall and as broad as a hundred-year-old oak tree. While Leaf's eyes are dark and soulful, Perry's are a light blue and full of mischief.

"Sure. You don't help with dinner service?"

He shakes his head. "Not unless I'm needed. Millie, Pete, and Leaf do the kitchen stuff, and once the lodge is busy, they hire students for the summer to help out. Which will be next week, come to think of it."

He motions for me to follow him and he explains how the lodge runs in slow times and off season. A skeleton staff can keep it running smoothly until it's booked to capacity for the summer. Next week the lodge will be half full and once July starts, it's full speed ahead.

We sit at a table together after visiting the buffet. Self-serve in low time is the norm and once we sit with our meal of mashed potatoes, carrots, and roast beef, Perry wastes no time interrogating me.

"What are your intentions with my brother?"

Coughing on my water at his directness, my eyes dart around to see if anyone is listening.

"Uh, he's a friend. We had a lovely time fishing. He's very welcoming."

Perry chews his food and considers my answer.

"Are you hoping to get into his bed?"

Sitting straighter, I meet his gaze.

"If you're implying I'm some bimbo here to score a quick fuck, you can kindly fuck off with that. And that's a grossly inappropriate question to ask me."

He doesn't apologize, but he does take his line of questioning down.

"My brother isn't someone to jump into bed with people. I don't want him hurt when you leave."

Cutting my roast beef with extra aggression, I try to think of what I want to say to Perry without being overly rude. I liked him earlier. He seemed like a fun guy but now he's a bit of an asshole.

"I've spent my whole life being judged. My appearance. My intelligence. My sexual habits. All of it. And if you must know, Leaf is the first person I've met in years—yes years, Perry—who hasn't judged me on any of those." Feeling the tears prick behind my eyes, I blink them back. "I appreciate you protecting your brother. It's quite noble, but maybe don't be such a prick when you barely know me."

So much for not being rude.

He has the good grace to lower his eyes, but I'm so upset I feel like stabbing his hand with my fork.

"I'm sorry."

My eyes snap to his and I hesitate, but he's sincere.

"Thank you. Apology accepted."

"You're not the first person to put me in my place. I tend to just say what's on my mind and it gets me in trouble. But... I know Leaf likes you. I'm just looking out for him."

"He likes me?"

"Yeah, like... wait, are you not interested in him?"

"Perry, with all due respect, I don't think it's any of your business. Brother or not, I barely know either of you."

"Is everything okay here?"

Leaf joins us and it doesn't escape me that he sits next to me and not Perry.

"I think we're good." Perry answers and his eyes plead with me to agree.

"Just peachy. Another amazing meal. I really must have Millie teach me some of this."

Leaf's smile could light up the dark side of the moon. Good lord my heart wants more than it came here for.

"She'd love to teach you. If you're serious, tomorrow might be a good day. But only if you want to. You're here for a vacation not to work."

"It's not work if I can get a cooking lesson or two thrown in."

"I'll leave you two to talk cooking. I'm heading home and I'll be back tomorrow. Unless you need me for anything else now, Leaf?"

The two brothers share a silent exchange before Leaf answers.

"Thank you for today. I'll see you tomorrow."

They fist bump and Perry clears his plate before stopping to talk with other tables of lodge patrons before leaving.

"I hope he wasn't mean to you. He's a nice guy, I promise. But since Connor died, he's like a mother bear sometimes. He means well."

Leaf's soft voice implies he knows exactly what Perry was grilling me on before he came to sit with us. His hopeful expression also sets me at ease.

"He wasn't very polite, but I think we have an understanding."

He nods as he eats, his shoulders relaxing.

"Good. He's my brother, and it's important to me that you like him."

"I guess I can understand that. I don't have any siblings, but if it's important to you, I'll respect that, and I'm sure we'll be fine."

He sets his fork down and turns to me.

"Do you have plans for tonight?" he blurts out like he's afraid he might change his mind if he doesn't talk fast. Laughing, I shake my head.

"A book and some tea unless you have wine stashed in these cabins I haven't found yet."

He inhales deeply before brushing his pinky finger over mine on the table.

"Would you like company? I'll bring wine."

Capturing his pinky with mine, I smile when his eyes light up.

"Make it a white one and it's a yes."

"I'll meet you at your cabin in an hour?"

He stands and takes away both of our plates while he waits for my answer.

"I'll see you then."

My eyes are on Leaf's back as he walks away, and I grip the table as I stand to steady my suddenly wobbly legs.

Chapter 6
Leaf

The wine I've chosen for my evening with Sasha sits on the counter. It's the last bottle I have in the place and he got lucky it just happens to be a white one. It was also one of Connor's favourites.

Staring at the bottle, I run a hand over my face.

"Con...I miss you, babe. So much."

It's a delicate decision. One I've always struggled with. When is it okay to allow myself to love another? Connor was such a huge part of my life, and even with him physically gone for seven years, he's always here to remind me of the happiness we shared.

Even in something as simple as a bottle of wine, the grief of what I lost rushes to the surface. It claws at my still-bruised heart like a thorn and rips open the wound like it was just yesterday.

But Sasha is so alive. He's a ray of sunshine and warm skin. He's the smile to my gloomy face when I wasn't looking for it.

And with him, I'm willing to try to move past the hump. This whole cloak of grief that still shadows even my best days can have an opening. A small step to the next part of my life, perhaps.

Or maybe just wine with a friend. Either one is a big move forward for me.

Tucking the bottle under my arm, I head to the kitchen, where I'm sure I'll still find Millie lingering. At least I hope to.

"Do you have a minute, Millie?"

She turns from the list she's making, a shopping list for the coming week, most likely.

"Always for you, Leaf." She motions to the bottle under my arm. "Are you planning to share that tonight?"

With a nod, I place it on the counter. Millie holds my gaze, waiting for more information.

"I miss him. Every day. That's nothing new. But I...I don't like being alone anymore, Mill."

She rests a hand on my arm. "You never have to be alone. He'd hate you being alone, you know. Connor was always the life of the party. He left a hole for you, and I know in my heart, Leaf, he'd want you to climb out of that hole and fill it up again."

Squeezing her hand, I sigh. The weight of it all clings to me so intimately, it's like a second skin.

"I just... why is it so hard?" Swallowing, I blink back the wetness that threatens to appear. "I really like Sasha. Connor would too, don't you think?"

She smiles. "He most definitely would. He'd ask him a million questions about photography and what magazines he'd been in. Then he'd ask him to Christmas dinner if he was free."

Huffing a little laugh, I grin. "And make sure he was included in the group photo before leaving with a plate of leftovers. But not with cookies, those were all for Connor."

There's so much I miss and still love about him. Talking with Millie eases my heart somewhat, but I need to know how to do this.

"I just asked if he had plans tonight and offered to bring wine if he didn't. And... the only bottle I had was Connor's favourite. It set me off. I mean, it's not like I'm asking him to marry me or anything. It's just some wine and conversation."

"Which is a perfect place to start, Leaf. He could be a friend you keep close or something more. You won't know until you try, and I think it's time to try."

She smoothes her hand on my arm. "You're the only one who needs to give yourself permission for this, Leaf. We all want you happy."

"You're right. Okay. I'm having wine with a friend tonight. Drive safe when you head out."

Kissing her cheek, I take the wine bottle and head out into the early summer evening toward Cabin Three. Dusk has arrived and with it, a few bullfrogs sing their songs to anyone listening. A pair of chipmunks race across my path, and I smile at their antics.

Cabin Three is in view and the lights inside shine bright. Sasha moves around in the living room and I wonder if he's already started to read the book he had planned for tonight. Maybe we like the same things. The only way I'll find out is if I move my feet and tell him I'm here, though. Step one is actually getting in the door.

Taking the steps up to the front porch, I knock once and he immediately opens the door with a smile. He's changed again, this time wearing a pair of silk pyjama pants that pool around his bare feet and a loose t-shirt.

"Hi. I thought you might have changed your mind."

My brow furrows.

"Why would you think that?"

"You said you'd be an hour, and it's closer to two. I just thought..." he smiles again. "I'm glad you're here now. Come in."

He steps back and I come inside, kicking my shoes off at the door.

"I'm sorry. I lost track of time. I... I needed to do some thinking."

"It's okay, Leaf. It's my insecurities getting the best of me, is all." He takes the wine to the kitchen and uncorks it like a pro while he speaks. "You know you have a corkscrew in here but no wine glasses. I hope a coffee mug is okay."

"I didn't know that. I'll see if I can get Pete to fix that for me and check the other cabins."

Sasha carries two mugs over with a bright smile, his pants swishing as he walks.

"I'm sure most people here don't prefer wine in the cabins. Besides, a mug is just as good. I'm not that posh. I'll drink it straight from the bottle if needed."

He passes me a mug. "Should we sit here or outside?"

"Here is fine."

Sasha takes one end of the sofa and I take the other. He tucks his legs up under him and sips the wine from the white *Corelle* mug. His smile is infectious and I return it before sipping my wine.

"This is really good. Where's it from?"

"It is. It's just a wine from one of the nearby vineyards. It was my husband's favourite."

Sasha holds my gaze and reaches a hand over to squeeze my leg.

"I'm sorry for your loss. It's easy to see you still love him very much. On the boat you had that faraway look when you spoke about him. The kind that swims with an ache for something in the past."

He gets it. Maybe more than some people.

"Have you ever lost someone? Someone who took a chunk of your heart and you were never sure if it could ever beat properly again?"

He smiles a wry smile before peering into his mug, and my heart stutters while I wait for his reply.

"We're just getting right into the heavy shit on our first night, are we?"

The silence hangs and I consider leaving. Maybe this isn't right. Connor's memory or not, perhaps Sasha isn't this beacon calling to me at all and it's just me being brave. But he shifts towards me.

"I have, yes. But not like you. My loss was a piece of me just the same, though."

"Sasha, I don't want to start this night off being a downer. I enjoy your company. You're attractive and I'm too old to fuck around with pretending. You're only here for a short time and I want to get to know you. I feel like you understand me more than most. That's why I asked."

He stares off out the window into the darkening evening. His profile is what I imagine photographers dream of. A straight jaw and nose, nice cheekbone definition, and gorgeous, plump lips.

I shift a little on the couch and discreetly adjust myself. He's very sexual without even trying. Perhaps that's part of his mystery.

"Leaf, you're not too old and I'm not too young. May I ask how old you are? I just turned twenty-eight."

"I'm forty-three. I lost my husband when I was thirty-six."

He sucks his bottom lip in before turning his gaze back to me.

"That's too young. Life isn't fair, right? We can go through the rest of our lives stewing in the melancholy of what we lost, always wondering why me, or we can move forward. We're still alive, Leaf. It might seem cruel to put it that way, but we're still here. Why should we punish ourselves for that?"

Sasha's warm gaze is like a soothing hand to a sore muscle. He may not want to share what happened to him, but there's no doubt he understands where I'm coming from.

"Human nature, I suppose. Guilt to still be here."

We both sip from our mugs, and Sasha shifts closer to me on the couch.

"Have you ever ridden a horse?"

His question throws me and I feel an unwilling smile on my lips.

"When I was just a kid. Some pony at the fair, I think."

"You should try it. Last summer I made a visit to the country and had a cowboy—a real one!—teach me to ride a horse. I'm an apartment-dweller, city kid, hate the dirt and outside. But I did it." He rests his arm across the back of the sofa. "It was the most freeing and exciting thing I'd ever done. Next to riding the mechanical bull."

Unbidden, I snort a laugh, picturing Sasha on a bull and I just can't. But when he smiles back over the top of his mug, his features are softer. Young and wise. A combination I wasn't expecting.

"The most freeing thing I've done was buy the 100 acres of maple trees up the road and start a maple syrup company." With a small laugh, I shake my head. "I didn't have a clue what to do. I just wanted to do it, you know?"

"I know." He murmurs, and in my heart, I know he means it. He does know.

"So what brought you to my lodge?"

The smile in my voice is genuine and I'm elated I came here tonight. Grateful that I took the step to get to know this charming man.

Sasha grins back, a flirty smile in place.

"To meet a lumberjack, of course." He sips from his mug with a wink, and I dip my head. A long-buried feeling courses through me. Excitement for this young, beautiful man. And lust. Bone deep lust for the warmth and coupling another body brings.

"Does it still count if I'm not a real one and only look like one?"

Sasha surprises me with a loud laugh. His eyes shine with amusement and I think... a soft affection.

"To be honest, I don't know what makes a real lumberjack. But you wear the plaid well. You probably use an axe well too, judging by your muscles." His eyes widen and he looks away.

I've not had this much fun with someone since, well, since I first met Connor. And damn, I've missed this.

"I thought it might be about the beard." I quip and a small laugh squeaks from Sasha.

"Yep. That too. Mhmm." He clears his throat. "But to answer your question, I came here to get away. To think about my future. A bit of soul searching, I guess." He sips his wine with a sigh. "I don't have many good memories of my mother, but the ones I do have involved us off-grid, camping or exploring where people couldn't find us. Watching the stars and sitting around campfires. Just simple shit."

There's a longing in his voice I recognize. A want for things to be like they were before. An easier time. A love that's missed, but not forgotten.

"You've come to the right place. It's pretty simple out here. I don't even have Wi-Fi."

"Which I should be more angry about because how can you run a business without it?"

"I don't know. I just do."

Sasha taps his mug with a finger. "Would you like a refill?"

Huh. I drain the last of the mug and pass it to him. "Sure. It's been a while since I've sat with a glass of wine and just talked to someone. If you don't mind me staying longer..."

Sasha holds my gaze. "Stay as long as you want."

He refills our cups, and while he's in the kitchen, I watch him move. He's more comfortable in the space than he was when he first arrived the other day. While his expensive silk pants seem out of place against the rough pine siding of the room, the man himself is not.

Before he sits back down, I stand as he offers me my mug back.

"Would you... do you want to see the stars?"

He blinks in surprise and tilts his head back.

"I'd love to. Now?"

"Is that okay?"

"I, uh, yeah. Let me get a sweater or something."

While he's getting what he needs, I swipe the blanket off the couch and meet him at the door.

"Do I need shoes?"

Smiling bigger than I have in years, I shake my head and pull off my socks.

"No." I reach for his hand as he laughs. "I promise you'll love this."

He smiles back. "Okay. I trust you."

And we disappear down to the beach.

Chapter 7
Sasha

Leaf tugs me behind him as we giggle, walking through the sand. Balancing coffee mugs of wine and not caring one bit if my silk pants fray, I make a note to never forget how carefree this moment is.

"I feel like a kid sneaking out after curfew." I laugh.

He slows down with a chuckle. "You're the only cabin out here until tomorrow. I don't know why I'm whispering."

My toes dig into the beach sand I had been expecting to be more rock than sand, but it's just as nice as any tropical beach I've been to. Although I could be distracted by the large, warm hand holding mine and not noticing much of anything else.

We stop short of the lake's edge and Leaf points to the sky with his free hand, careful to not slosh his wine too much.

"There's no better time to star gaze than on a clear night over a lake. If you love stars, you'll love this."

Tilting my head back, I survey the sky. The stars shine brighter than any diamond in the coal-black night. It feels like the night sky is a piece of dark paper pulled tight and the stars shining through are lights from another world. We're just two tiny specks in a terrarium.

"It's beautiful out here."

He releases my hand and shakes out the blanket he had slung over his arm.

"If you lay down, you won't hurt your neck."

He lies down and pats the blanket next to him and holds out his hand. Smiling and bubbling with excitement, I lie down beside him. Shoulders brushing together, we stare up at the sky.

Leaf points out constellations and I listen to the low rumble of his words and sneak glances at his lips. Deciding to focus on the sky rather than the enchanting man next to me, my mind wanders.

His shoulder nudges mine, and the edge of his hand gently caresses mine on the blanket between us.

"Hey, are you okay? You got really quiet. I'm sorry if I got all boring with my astronomy stuff."

"Sorry, I was thinking. You're not boring. Not even a little."

We stare up at the sky and I carefully find his hand between us and lay mine on top of his. He turns his hand so his large fingers wrap around my smaller ones. It's a small gesture in the grand scheme of things, but my hand in his grounds me here.

We don't speak because we don't have to. There's both a familiar comfort to his presence and a big, scary thing I don't want to name. Because it wasn't my intention to come here and form an emotional connection with someone. A friend, sure, but Leaf is different. While he's looking to move on from a huge loss, I'm not sure I can do the same just yet. But he's intuitive and we get each other. The words don't need to be spoken. It's hard to ignore how easily we seem to slide into each other's lives.

"I should probably head home. The new lodgers are arriving tomorrow. You'll see a lot more people around."

"No rest for the owner, I guess."

"I'll be busier, but the evenings are usually free. I'd like to spend more time with you if I can."

Swallowing, I turn my head to find Leaf watching me. Soulful brown eyes that see me more than anyone has, wait with the hope I won't say no. Of course, I can't say no.

"I'd like that very much."

He nods, getting up off of the blanket, while I do the same. Leaf shakes the sand out and together we walk back to my cabin.

The light inside glows through the window and, once inside, Leaf grabs his socks and sits on the edge of the sofa.

"If you want to go into town tomorrow, Pete is dropping people off in the morning and heading back. Catch him before he leaves, around 9 A.M.. I guarantee he'd love to give you a tour."

"Oh, thanks. That would be great."

He stands at the door after tying his shoes, rocking awkwardly onto his heels.

"Thank you for this, Sasha. I had a nice time."

"I did too. Thank you for the wine and... everything."

"You're welcome. I'll let you get some reading done. Goodnight."

He lets himself out, and I return to the sofa with a sigh.

This was not part of my plan.

After breakfast, I did as Leaf suggested and flagged Pete down, hitching a ride into the town of Maple.

On a school bus.

"You'll like Maple, Sasha. I know you're from the city and probably miss a lot of the comforts, but Maple has culture."

Pete lifts his chin, proud of his town, daring me to disagree.

"I bet it does, Pete. Tell me what I should see. How long do I have?"

The bus grinds and shudders as he turns off the dirt road from the lodge onto the paved highway. The town is in the opposite direction of the service station he picked me up at.

"I have a group of people to pick up at 3 P.M.. I can swing up here to get you before then. How about I pick you up outside the coffee shop at 2:45 P.M.?"

"Oh! A coffee shop? Yes! That sounds great."

"The people who run it are very friendly. I'll drop you there first so you know where to find me."

"Do you have a cell phone? Just in case I get lost or something?"

He booms a laugh as he pulls the bus into a parking lot to turn around.

"I don't need those things." He passes me a business card for the lodge. "If anything comes up, call the lodge direct. Ask for me or Leaf, and we'll help." He points to a very modern building. The outside is grey brick with a sleek black trim. There's a full-size canoe on the storefront with the words '*Ragged Chutes Coffee House*', written using pieces of driftwood.

"That's the coffee shop. I'll park in this lot. If I'm not in the bus, I'll be in there getting a coffee and a cookie. Try their salted caramel brownie if it's out."

"I will! Is everything on this street, then? I can walk to everything?"

Pete explains how small the town really is, but everything I need is literally in the four blocks of downtown. Slinging my camera bag over my chest, I head into the coffee shop first.

The first thing I notice is the sign that announces free Wi-Fi with a password.

"Good morning, sugar. What can I get you?"

The young man behind the cash can't be much older than me. He's just as tall and broad as Leaf, but without the beard. Just a baby face smile and a pair of the bluest eyes I've ever seen.

"Do you have any salted caramel brownies today? Pete told me to ask."

"Ah, Pete. He's a good guy. You must be staying at the lodge then."

He places the brownie in a cellophane bag and I order one of their house coffees with a name I can't turn down: *Chute me with Caffeine.*

"Yes, I'm at the lodge and my first shock was the lack of cell coverage and internet. Your Wi-Fi sign is a godsend."

The man chuckles as he slides a sleeve on my takeout cup.

"*Heh*, yeah. We need it here. How else can I stalk celebrities online and know what my best friend ate for lunch?"

Snorting, I laugh as I pay. "That's the truth. I need to let my friend know I haven't been eaten by a bear yet. I'm going to enjoy this brownie, catch up on messages, and then I might ask you about the town if that's okay?"

"Sure thing. Enjoy."

Settling into the corner and out of the way of patrons, I open my phone and log into the shop's Wi-Fi. My phone buzzes with emails and text notifications and while it catches up on downloading them all, I bite into the brownie and it's like a bar of orgasms. My lord, there's never been a better brownie in my mouth. I'll have to get one for Pete. Assuming I can get it to him without eating it first, that is.

But first, a chat with Roman is what I need.

He's only left me three texts since he knows I have sketchy cell service, but a quick check of my phone shows me I have four bars in town. So that's a pleasant change from the lodge's reception, but for now I'll text him in between emails.

I may not be on contract as a model with anyone anymore, but I still do freelance work if it's a job I feel comfortable with. While booking a month off was risky for those one-off appearances, it was much-needed and a risk I was willing to take.

> **Sasha:** I'm exploring the little town here today. Still no bears of either kind.

Chuckling at my own joke, I sip the coffee, and it's just as good as the brownie. I would totally replace Starbucks with this place.

Opening my email I groan at the number of unopened ones and wonder how many are actually important and how many are from friends of my slimeball ex-agent, Moe.

Seven is the correct answer. Moe's allies have emailed me seven times in three days and it's always the same crap. I'm not going back.

Not as a friend, a client, or a lover.

> **Roman:** Dang. I'd go for the two-legged kind. How's the hot lumberjack you met? See any hardwood, yet? Get it? Wood! I kill me.

> **Sasha:** Your attempt at humour kills me.

> **Roman:** I'm funny and you love me.

Sasha: True. I do love you. But work on the comedy.

Roman: So… lumberjack, what happened?

Good question. Nothing happened really, but it felt like everything. Or the start of something? I used to be confident in my decisions and my ability to read people, but Moe left a sour taste in my mouth and my confidence shaken.

Sasha: He's nice.

Roman: Nice? Suede is nice. Not a hot dude wearing flannel.

Roman: BTW, did Moe the idiot email you? Not his friends. Him.

I've deleted a few emails and was about to delete the ones from Moe's friends, but Roman's question stops me. Scrolling, I find one from Moe himself. When I read the email, my hands curl into tight balls, fingernails biting into my skin.

Sasha: I just read it. Can he do that?

Roman: I'll ask my lawyer. You just enjoy the away time and don't feel guilty, okay? You're not letting him bring you down farther.

Moe is a bastard of the highest order. He wants to sue me for breaking my contract last year when I broke my arm. Even though he fired me and broke the partnership himself, I was stupid and have no physical proof. He claims I didn't show up for work and cost him several hundred thousand dollars in lost revenue. He threatens me with this after I found a bank statement that clearly shows he's been stealing from me for years.

At first I was worried he'd blacken my name in the fashion world and no one would want to hire me. But it was the opposite. Once he was no longer my agent, more offers were made to me. Moe didn't like that he had no control over me anymore. He was afraid I'd talk. And I did. He stole more than just money from me. When I confessed to a friend in law enforcement about what Moe had done, she had me in front of a lawyer, spilling my guts.

He abused me and my trust for too long. I was willing to walk away and forget, but he crossed a line that I was afraid to speak to anyone about. Sex with a minor is frowned upon, especially when he was supposed to be my guardian.

Sasha: I'll try to. Leaf will be busy this week, so I'm not sure how much of him I'll see. But there's a bookstore across the street and I'm going there next.
I'll enjoy my time here. It's a beautiful town.

> **Roman:** I should probably get out of bed, too. Keep in touch. I already miss you!

After signing off with Roman, I get the young man's attention at the cash.

"Is there a place that prints photos here? From a memory card?"

"Yeah! The pharmacy on the next block over has a machine near the greeting card section. I've used it a few times, decent quality."

"And where is the best place for groceries?"

The young man holds up a finger and disappears briefly in the back room. When he returns, he holds a map and a booklet.

"I've been meaning to get a little holder for these. I often get people here asking the same questions." He flips open the map and circles the places I'm asking about. "You won't get lost. And if you need a place to drop some bags off while you wait for Pete to return, I'd be happy to do that for you."

"Oh! Thank you! That would be wonderful." I hold out my hand. "I'm Sasha by the way."

He grins and takes my hand in a sure grip. "I'm Caleb. This is my shop. Well, my dad and I own it together. He's the one that made the brownies."

"You've been so helpful, Caleb. Thank you."

Stepping out into the late morning sun, I walk the path Caleb highlighted to reach the pharmacy first. A small bridge spans the river that snakes through town and I pause at the side, staring down the lush green slopes of the river banks. It's just as serene here as it is at the lodge.

I'm about to keep walking when a family of ducks swims out from under the bridge and I can't wipe the sappy smile off my face at the fuzzy ducklings. It reminds me of a park my mom used to take me to. We'd feed the ducks our bread crusts, even though we weren't supposed to. I even petted them a few times. When I was older and learned bread wasn't good for them, it broke my heart, but at the time it was one of the happiest things we did.

Once they've swum out of sight, I keep walking. The beautiful street is lined with flower boxes and hanging planters from every light post. Storefronts are old stone or brick with old-fashioned wooden signage. It's quaint and warm, like a quilt someone's grandma made.

The pharmacy surprises me. There's nothing sterile about the place. The door jingles when I step inside. A faint odour of lemon *Pinesol* still lingers from last night's cleaning and a country music station plays softly. The card row is easy to spot and there at the end is the photo kiosk.

"Can I help you with anything?"

An older gentleman with greyish hair and a kind smile pokes his head out from behind a one-way mirror.

"Oh! You scared me." I laugh. "I'm just here to print some photos."

He smiles and nods. "Not many people print them anymore. It's all digital this, cloud that. Nothing beats seeing that photo in a frame or in your wallet, though."

Unable to help myself, I nod and agree.

"Exactly! Sure a photo fades, but pinning that photo of your crush to your pillow? You can't do that with a phone."

He cocks his head with a chuckle. "You don't look old enough to talk about pinning photos to pillow cases, son."

Dipping my head, the heat flooding my neck, I nod.

"My mom always said I had an old soul." Clearing my throat, I gesture to the machine. "I'll just get started then."

After popping my memory card in the slot and picking out far too many favourites, I quickly crop a few and send them to print. While the machine spits out the photos, I browse the cards and find one to send to Roman and, after a slight hesitation, I choose one for Leaf.

I know he said he'd be busy this week, but it wouldn't hurt to remind him I'm here.

At least, I think so. I know I wasn't coming here to get involved with someone, but if we have a connection, why shouldn't I nurture it?

With that thought in my head, I pay and leave the drugstore so I can get to the grocery store before I run out of time. I don't want to keep Pete waiting, and I need snacks for the cabin.

Chapter 8
Leaf

I've forgotten how easy it is to get swept up into the activities at the lodge once it's booked full. Between checking people in, overseeing the kitchen, and making sure all the guests have the guides they requested, I'm exhausted.

I don't *have* to check on Millie in the kitchen—she's more than capable—but it makes me feel useful. I don't really have to do any of it. I can assign most of these things to someone else. But it kept me busy after Connor died, and I've just never changed my ways.

It's not until midweek I remember the envelope on my kitchen table. Sasha left it with Millie after he helped cook breakfast one morning. I wanted to stay and watch him laugh. His eyes twinkled with delight as he and Millie chattered like old friends. He didn't know a lick about cooking, but he paid attention and did his best.

And it wasn't lost on me the way my heart squeezed while I watched him with my mother figure. The pull of wanting a new life was strong.

Carefully opening the flap of the envelope, I pull out the card inside and catch the photo that tumbles out. It's the one I took of Sasha on the boat with his first fish and his smile disarms me now, just like it did then.

A beautiful man out of his normal element, yet still thriving. Wearing my old thrift store shirt over his designer clothes and holding a wiggly fish with his soft, manicured hands.

The card is simple. A photo of a nightscape and star-filled sky is on the front. Inside is a handwritten note.

Leaf,

I've not been here long and you've already shown and taught me so much. I can't put into words how much catching this fish means to me, but know that it's special. I'll never forget this experience. Or you.

Sasha

"You aren't easy to forget either, city boy."

The clock reads half past ten at night. I know I need to be at the docks for a 6 A.M. fishing group, but I miss Sasha. It's silly and weird, but it's there.

"Connor, wherever you are, if you can hear me..." My eyes water and I blink furiously. "I love you. And I'm going to try to do this again. If not with Sasha, maybe the next one who gives me those same butterflies. Because if someone can make me feel the way you did, I want that again. Very much."

Wiping at my eyes, I lay the photo of Sasha on the table. The part nobody warns you about when you lose your spouse is the guilt you feel for loving someone new. Not that I love Sasha, but he's stoked the fire to love again.

And I'd be lucky to have it twice in my life. What Connor and I had was magic like nothing else. Since he's been gone, I've been hollow. Going through the motions and staying alone when I can. Millie, Pete, and even my brother, Perry, have all assured me it's normal. But they've also gently reminded me Connor would never want me to be like this.

They're right.

Without giving myself time to overthink it, I exit my suite and head down the path to Cabin Three.

My heart pounds in my throat the closer I get, and I pause when I notice the light on inside. He's still awake. Lightly, I climb the steps to his door and knock. My heart's in my throat and sweaty palms stuffed deep in my pockets.

And there he is.

Damp and tussled hair, a rosy glow on his cheeks from maybe too much sun today and his lips part in surprise before turning up in a happy smile.

"Leaf. Hi. Do you want to come in?"

Nodding, I step inside. My whole body warms like coals on a fire once I step past him. Tiny sleep shorts and a crop top are his nighttime outfit and it's the first time I've seen this much of his toned body.

"I hope it's not too late to drop by."

"No. I was just reading and thinking of opening more potato chips." He pats his flat stomach with a chuckle. "I can eat all the junk food here and nobody cares. It's been great. I just hope I still fit into my clothes after."

He resumes his place on the couch, tucking his slender legs under him, and pats the space in invitation. Kicking off my shoes, I settle on the other end.

The book he's reading sits between us and I reach for it. "May I? Is this what you're reading?"

"It is. I hope to finish it tonight. It's beautiful. The cover caught my eye, and the story is... hopefully romantic."

The cover is a younger man with a wet white shirt plastered to his torso. Maybe caught in a rainstorm since the title is *Too Like the Lightning*. The man's eyes are obscured, but his full lips are turned up in a smile. Maybe at the man he's in love with? A quick browse at the book's synopsis has a lump form in my throat.

He didn't plan on making a friend. Suddenly the long summer seems far too short.

With a trembling hand, I place the book back on the cushion. This story sounds far too much like my reality with Sasha.

"What do you like about it?"

"The story?" He takes the book and flips through the pages. A small lift of his lip as he stops on the bookmarked page. "It's full of hope. And finding yourself. And maybe reaching for something you think is impossible." He licks his lips and meets my gaze. "Being brave."

The silence rests between us as he flits his fingers across the cover.

"I wanted to thank you for the card and the picture. It turned out nice. I would've come sooner but..." Swallowing hard, I laugh. It's dry and tinged with embarrassment. "I, ah, forgot to open it when Millie gave it to me. I've just been so busy–"

He places his hand on my thigh. "It's okay. I get it. You're here now and I'm glad you liked it. I guess that was me being brave. I wasn't sure what you'd think of it."

Him being brave? Is he reaching for what he thinks is impossible? Does he think I'm out of his league or is he also thinking of how little time we have left to be together?

"I've not stopped thinking about you since that night." My voice is thick and heavy as I confess to him he's been on my mind.

Turning to face him, I'm again struck by his youthful beauty. So simple and fresh. Maybe unsullied by life on the outside, though he did mention he'd suffered losses, too. He must hide his scars behind his smiles better than most.

His throat bobs with a swallow and his lips part with a small huff.

"Leaf?" Sasha places the book on the side table. His hand trembles and he shimmies closer to me. "You're *all* I've been thinking about."

It's right there; his upturned face and little nose. Those parted pink lips waiting for mine. A longing in his eyes that's not just lust. That's there, but there's something else that speaks to my broken heart.

Sliding my palm across his cheek, I gather my own courage.

"I'd like to be brave with you. Even if it's only a short time, Sasha. I don't know what the future brings or if we go beyond tonight, but... there's something about you I can't ignore."

"You're not like anyone I've ever met." His hand slides up my chest. "We can be brave together. Sometimes the first step leads to great things."

We've drifted closer, our noses brush, and his short breaths warm me further on the hot summer night. And for the first time in seven years, I kiss someone.

Pressing my lips to his, my body trembles with the enormity of this step. He tastes like salt and Diet Coke and his lips are softer than a goose's down. Licking across his lips, his tongue meets mine, eager and gentle. I expected a wildcat of a response from him. Someone worldly and sex-filled who takes charge. But his body vibrates just like mine, a nervous thrum, and I pull him onto my lap.

His hands grip my shoulders and he gasps when my hands slide under his tiny top.

Nuzzling his neck, I inhale his scent. Jasmine maybe, it's sweet and light and perfect for him. His body sags against me as my long-slumbering libido wakes. I want him more than my next breath.

He grinds into my lap, hard and needy, as his hands drift to the buttons on my shirt.

Our kisses grow, overflowing with a passion that drowns out any of the doubt remaining that I should do this. I remove his speck of a shirt with ease and he sits on my lap, panting with lips swollen and slicked with our saliva.

"Sasha..."

My voice cracks and I'm not sure what I want to say. There're so many emotions swirling inside me, so many thoughts and my tongue only wants to taste him.

He shakes his head and slides my shirt off my shoulders. "Don't. Please. Can we just pretend the summer will never end and we're the only two people in the world?"

A flash of sadness crosses his face. My heart yearns to take it away. To wipe away anything that doesn't make him smile.

"Yeah," my voice rumbles, thick with desire. "I'd like that."

His fingers feather and dance across my chest, teasing over my nipples and smoothing across my abdomen. My breath hitches with each touch. It feels so good to have warm hands on my skin and lips on mine. A body to hold. Someone to share pleasure with.

Someone to make me feel alive again.

My mind spins like a pinwheel in a windstorm. Where do I start? My dick screams that it wants it all. And now. Standing with him in my arms, he squeaks with surprise. I lay him gently on the couch and blanket my body over his.

My beard leaves a strawberry trail across his pale flesh as I head toward the waistband of his skimpy shorts. Slender, but strong fingers brush through my hair and his nails scrape my scalp. A guttural groan leaves my lips.

His back arches and I slide his shorts down his legs. Now completely naked under me, I'm once again frozen. Every damn molecule of him is beautiful. From his charming smile to his slender feet.

My hand shakes as I run it up his thigh.

"Sasha..."

He reaches for me and cradles my face in his palms. His fingers slide into my beard and he leans forward to press his lips softly to mine.

"It's hard for me to trust people, Leaf." His breath stutters and he opens his eyes. "But I trust you. Please be gentle with me."

His chest heaves as he stares at me, naked and so vulnerable.

"Did someone hurt you, Sasha?"

He shakes his head, far too quickly for my comfort.

"Not... not like that." He swallows hard and pulls me closer. "I trust you. Please."

A moment passes and my heart goes all kinds of haywire. How could he be hurt so badly that he has to beg me to be gentle? Or does he mean something else? Whatever it is, I know in my bones I would cherish this man more than life itself if he were mine.

"Are you okay here, or do you want the bed? Or the floor?" I smile, thinking of the floor when we're surrounded by comfortable furniture and I'm rewarded with a smile back. His shine returns and he sits up, hard cock bouncing against his stomach.

"First, you need to be naked. And right here is fine with me."

We smile and fumble through my clothes. I seem to be wearing too many for a summer night, and once I'm just as naked as he is, he presses against me.

We move in sync. Painfully perfect as we read each other's sighs and movements like we lived it before. Maybe even rehearsed it.

We're gentle caresses and demanding pulls. Exploring tongues and breathy moans. Each of us hungry for the other in a way I've never experienced before.

We haven't even laid back down and we're racing towards mutual orgasms standing naked in the tiny living area of Cabin Three.

"I'm gonna come, Leaf."

Sasha groans and bites into my shoulder as he sags into me, still thrusting through my loose grip on his cock. His whole body jolts and heaves, and a small cry crosses his lips as he spills into my fist.

"Are you okay?" Hugging him closer, not caring about the cum on my hand, I pry his face away from my shoulder.

He shakes his head again, fighting free, and kisses my neck. His hand still on my dick, he brings me to the edge and I free fall off it. My chest tightens with an abundance of emotions as I clutch him closer to me and spill into his hand with a full body shudder.

Transcendental isn't the right word. But it's close. This wasn't a one-night stand. There's so much more here crackling under the surface. It scares the shit out of me, but it also excites me—the possibilities we could have with our limited time.

Our ragged pants fill the room and he squeezes onto me harder. Like he's afraid I might evaporate before his eyes if he lets go.

"Can I help you with a shower, babe?"

He lifts his head from my shoulder, and his sweet smile is a direct hit.

"I'd like that. Can you stay?"

I know I'll be dragging my ass once 5 A.M. rolls around, but something happened here tonight and I'm not ready to leave it.

"I will."

Chapter 9
Sasha

Leaf and I laid awake most of the night talking.

Actual conversation.

Sure hands and lips wandered some too, but there was an inherent shift in our new friendship.

For one thing, we went beyond friends. And I didn't hate it.

Quite the opposite. I liked it so much I already know it's going to hurt like nothing I've ever felt before when I have to leave.

If Leaf hadn't shown up last night, my plan was to finish my book and go into town early for more exploring. Instead, I slept in and barely managed to get a ride with Pete in the afternoon. I brought my camera and phone with the sole purpose of finding a bench in the tiny park I saw to call Roman in a mostly private setting.

The gods are on my side today. The park is quiet and a bench under a giant maple tree is free. Ducks swim by in small groups and I swear it's the same ones making a loop somehow. They're turning around down stream and sneaking back without me noticing. They have to be.

But this park grounds me, even with the endless duck loop, and I hope like hell Roman isn't in the middle of a photo shoot so we can talk.

"Sasha! Hi!"

His smiling voice is just what I needed to hear.

"Hey, Ro. Do you have a few minutes to talk? I, uh, I need you."

Roman's voice is muffled before he comes through again, this time softer and not the larger-than-life guy most people know.

"Hey, Sash. I'm alone now. Are you okay?"

Running my hand through my hair, I sigh a shaky breath.

"Ro, fuck, so much has happened the last few days."

I feel the tickle in my nose as the tears threaten and blink them away.

"Leaf. I...he came over and..." A hard swallow, then another. "He spent the night."

Roman doesn't need details. He knows how huge this is for me without spelling it out.

"Oh, sweetie. What happened? Did you tell him about you?"

"I told him it's hard for me to trust. We talked for hours and he knows Moe was my guardian and took advantage of me."

Rowan sucks in a breath. "How did he respond?"

"Not well. I imagine if Moe had been close, he'd be in a million tiny pieces right now."

"Okay, that's good, though. He's on your side. But... did you, ah, actually sleep together?"

Roman knows since I spent so many years naïve about the modelling business, believing Moe when he manipulated me into sex with people for contracts, that I had a hard time processing it all. Including intimacy.

Sex was great, but after that time in my life, casual encounters were no longer my thing. I was paranoid and detached from reality. I didn't want to give myself to anyone in exchange for anything that had a monetary value. There's nothing wrong with sex work when you do it of your own volition, but I was unwittingly forced into it. My inexperience with life was my downfall, or I'd have noticed sooner. But when you place your trust in someone and they use that against you, it does a number on your thought processes.

It took me years of therapy to accept I was more than a bargaining chip. But sometimes those insecurities burst to the surface again and shake up my thoughts.

"We did. And I trusted him, Roman. Fuck, I didn't question his motives a single time. But I told you Leaf was a widower, right? I think he understands my hang-ups because of that. He shared about his husband, too."

"This all sounds great. But what are you worried about?"

"I only have another fourteen days here." Gulping hard, I know it will pass far too quickly. "In fourteen days, I won't get to see him again."

He hums and I feel his patronizing look over the phone.

"Sasha. You know you can see him again if you choose. You can work anywhere, darling. Don't feed me bullshit and call it dinner. Tell me the truth."

Laughing softly, I curse my friend for knowing me so well.

"I don't know if I want to love someone. Leaf gets it; he's lost a spouse. I've lost my mom and have no blood family. I just... I don't know! I don't know why I'm scared. He's so different, Roman. And I've never, ever felt like this before. It's like he's too good to be true."

A duck quacks and despite my turmoil, it makes me smile to watch them swim by.

Again.

It's the same group. It has to be.

"Sasha, you deserve good things, babe. We all do. Life is too damn short. If the next fourteen days make you wish you could never leave, I suggest you hold on to that and figure out how to stay there. Don't let it pass you by."

A group of teenagers have now wandered into the park and are loud enough that I don't want to say much more in case they overhear.

"Listen, I'll think about it. I'm gonna let you go. I love you, my friend. I'll check in again soon."

Pocketing my phone, I silently curse Roman for being so obvious and in my face. Smug bastard. But I can't ignore his advice.

With only forty minutes to spare before Pete picks me up, I amble back towards the main street, intent on dropping in the bookstore for a quick peek.

"Excuse me," one of the teenagers calls out and I turn. "Are you... Sasha Montpellier?"

The young girl holds her breath, and her three friends wait behind her.

"I am."

They all erupt at once.

"OHMYGOD!"

"I knew it was him!"

"This is so fucking awesome!"

A bit overwhelmed, I hold up my hands for quiet. "Ah, I'm at a loss here. You all know me and I don't know your names."

The leader of the group holds out a sharpie and a magazine. And it clicks. The spread I did in *Teen VOGUE*, the teenage version of *VOGUE*. They recognize me. I'm used to being noticed only for my looks and not my actual identity. It's usually, *'oh it's the guy from the billboard* or *the guy from the underwear ad'*. For someone to call *my* name out is a nice surprise.

"I'm Violet and these are my friends, Mitchell, and Sparrow."

Taking her magazine and *Sharpie* I scrawl a short message and my name at the top of the spread.

"So, what did you think of this piece?"

Mitchell, the lone boy in the group, nods his head. "The interview was awesome. I think you're very courageous."

Glancing down at the article, my bright pink cast blazes on the crisp magazine page. It was my last contracted modelling gig under Moe. It wasn't supposed to be an interview, but when they heard my story of being fired and *why* I rode a mechanical bull, they changed their plans. It was the first time I went public with any of my issues and, since it was a magazine aimed at teenagers, I wanted them to know it's okay to question adults and to listen when friends voice concerns.

Of course, Moe was furious and threatened me with a lawsuit if I painted him in a negative light, so we kept that part in the background as best we could. However, the rest of the interview talked about my struggle with modelling, my issues with a personal identity, and the reality of being turned into a sex symbol before I knew what sex was. It was the first time I spoke publicly about any of it.

"Thank you. I'm happy that the message reached you."

"How come you're in our tiny town, Sasha?"

Violet folds the magazine carefully and presses it to her chest.

"Well... a vacation. You have a lovely town."

"Would you ever come back here? Our drama club has open nights and it would be so cool if you could come." Sparrow, a tiny waif of a thing, speaks in a voice larger than her body.

"I'm not into acting. I just pose for cameras." I hold up my camera case. "I love photography, though."

"Our teacher told us drama class isn't always about learning a part in a play. It's finding out your strengths and what you're capable of. It's overcoming fears."

Sparrow's eyes speak to something beyond those words, and I find myself nodding.

"Your teacher is right. If I come back, I'll think about it. I do like it here."

"There's only one high school. The information is on the *Facebook* page. It's easy to find if you change your mind. We meet during the summer, without a teacher. Some of us need it."

Mitchell looks away after that comment and my heart aches for whatever he's going through.

"I'll do that. I need to get going. It was so nice to meet you all."

"Wait!" Sparrow pulls out her phone. "Can we get a few photos?"

Squishing all together, she snaps a few selfies and I leave them to sort through all the photos we took. With only twenty minutes until Pete returns, I change course and head to the drugstore photo booth again.

After eating dinner in the lodge, I head back to my cabin alone. Leaf was busy being host, but he smiled and waved as he tended to his guests. Not wanting to interrupt his flow, I left quietly, completely stuffed with Millie's lasagna.

After slipping into a pair of lounge pants and a t-shirt, I light the citronella candle on the porch and make myself comfortable on the porch swing. The moon is bright tonight, but I have a book light and with a fuzzy blanket tucked over me, I let the swing sway as I turn the pages of another romance book.

I'm not sure how I started reading these kinds of books. Perhaps it was when I was looking for proof that relationships could be full of tenderness and real love. Or most likely, the cover was something to catch my eye. My read tonight is titled *The Cockpit*, and the dreamy silver fox of a man on the front had me reach for my wallet without even reading what it was about.

More than once, my hand wiped away the wetness on my cheeks while reading about the thoughtful gestures by each of the characters. Do men like this actually exist? Could Leaf surprise me with love letters if I went away with the promise to return?

The night grows late, and it's after midnight when I place my bookmark and stare out at the calm lake. Most of the lodgers get up at the crack of dawn for fishing trips or hiking excursions. It's quiet because they all went to bed hours ago and I wish so badly for Leaf to appear again. If I knew where the entrance to his suite was, I'd go knock on his door and hand deliver the next card and photo I printed for him right now.

Rising with my book and blanket, I blow out the candle and pause when I hear footsteps drawing closer.

And there he is.

"Is it too late to come in?"

Leaf stands in the shadows off the porch and the sound of his voice wraps around me like a hug I so desperately want.

"No." I breathe. "I was just heading in myself."

When he steps closer, my gaze drops to his hands, and he puffs an awkward breath.

"I wanted to bring you flowers, but I couldn't get away to go into town in time to do it. Then I wanted to bring you some of your favourite potato chips, but we were out." He steps closer and thrusts his hand forward. "So I picked some daisies from the field across the road, and I hope you like them."

The flowers shake in his grasp as he waits for my response. Swallowing the sudden lump in my throat, I step towards him.

"Thank you." I take the four spindly stocks with their missing petals and blotchy yellow centers and let the wetness freely spill down my cheeks.

"They're perfect, Leaf. Really."

"Don't cry, Sasha." Large thumbs wipe my cheeks. "I don't know what I'm doing, but I know I don't want to see you cry."

Could he be more romantic without even trying? My gentle giant bringing me flowers and wiping my tears because I'm a hot mess of emotions over it and he doesn't even blink an eye at my response.

"Do any of us really know what we're doing?"

"I don't think so, no."

"Can you stay again? All night?"

He nods and reaches for my free hand.

"Yeah. I can." He dips his head. "I mean, I was hoping to."

"I was hoping you'd come. I don't know how to get to your place or I would have gone to you. I was just thinking of that and then you showed up like you heard my wish."

His mouth ticks up in a small smile.

"Really? Well, why don't you come home with me in the morning and I'll show you my place."

"I'd like that."

His eyes are brighter than the moon's glow, and his smile is genuine. Can I let myself believe this man might be what I've yearned for and we can make something out of whatever it is that's brewing between us?

When I close the door behind us, a seed of hope takes root.

Chapter 10
Leaf

The morning sun shines through the crack in the curtains far too soon and I gaze at Sasha next to me. Our legs tangled together and his head on my chest feels good.

So damn good.

I knew I missed Connor and his physical presence, but I didn't notice how much I missed another person in their entirety. A warm leg pressed against mine, a breath on my chest in the dark. Conversation in bed and the knowledge that I won't be eating breakfast alone is suddenly incredibly enticing.

Old feelings and new ones are tumbling together and I know I need to do good by Sasha while balancing my memories of Connor.

It's not easy.

But my friends and family are right. I know I shouldn't spend the rest of my life alone. Connor would one hundred percent hate that I'm cooping myself up and not laughing. And I know he'd be disappointed I let the sugar shack and maple syrup slide.

Sasha stirs next to me and his long eyelashes flutter open.

"What time is it?"

"Does it matter?"

He tilts his head back to look at me. "Don't you need to be at the lodge to help for breakfast and excursions and stuff?"

"Mmm, technically yes, but they already know what needs to be done if I'm late."

Sasha pushes up with a smile.

"You're staying with me all day?"

Rolling over, I pin him underneath me. His smile and laugh make my heart beat out of time. "I'm definitely not rushing out."

Leaning down, I brush my lips across his, and he sighs.

"A guy could get used to this in the morning."

Humming in agreement, I flutter kisses along his jaw and neck. "A guy definitely could. How do you taste so sweet all the time?"

He slides his hands down my back and drags his nails down my spine. When I shiver and groan, he laughs again. It's so carefree and so... alive.

Fuck. I've been dead right along with Connor this whole time.

I've missed this so much. It's only now by letting someone else touch me and make me smile, I feel the weight I've been carrying.

It's heavy and I'm so tired of it crushing the air from my lungs. But it's not as easy as just waking up and flipping a switch. No matter how beautiful and happy that switch is.

"Leaf? Are you okay?"

Sasha's gentle voice pulls me out of my thoughts.

"I don't want to hurt you."

His smile fades, and he passes his hand over my cheek.

"Then don't."

Staring into his eyes that say so much that his lips don't, I drop my forehead to his.

"Can I take you somewhere today?"

"Of course. What did you have in mind?"

Rolling back to my side, I take his hand in mine. My thumb dusts across his knuckles while I gather my thoughts.

"I think you've already been there. But I want to show it to you and tell you what happened. I want to take you to my sugar shack. Where I used to make maple syrup... it's what brought me to this mountain."

"I'd love to. And yes, I did go once. That's where Perry found me when he drove me back that day. I don't know anything about maple syrup except I know I love to eat it." He smiles brightly and again I'm sucked into his charm. His light ways that are so appealing even when I know he carries his own scars.

"Good. I... well, there's lots for me to tell you. How about I snag some food from the kitchen and we spend the day there?

Then if you'd like, you could have dinner with me. In my place, not the lodge."

Sasha's eyes widen, and he stumbles over his words.

"I'd, yeah, that sounds... heh, should we get up and get started then?"

"Yeah, let's do it."

He bounces out of bed and I'm gifted with the view of his firm ass as he walks to the bathroom. Unbidden, my lips turn into a satisfied smile. Over his shoulder, Sasha catches me watching.

"I see you." He winks. "I like that you like it."

The bathroom door closes and I stare up at the ceiling. I'm really doing this. Sasha will know everything about Leaf, the lodge owner, former maple syrup producer, and widowed recluse.

And if I'm lucky, maybe a bit of the romantic he so desperately craves. If I'm super lucky, maybe he'll see the Leaf I used to be.

Sasha's hair peeks out from under his ATV helmet as we whiz along the road to the sugar shack. He clutches his camera bag to his chest with one hand and has a death grip on the *holy shit* bar above his head.

But he's smiling. His nervous laughter when we hit a bump is something I wish I could bottle.

Gearing down, I turn us onto to the long and winding road up to the sugar shack. My heart breaks when I notice the sign is all rusted and broken. When I first placed that sign in the ground, it was the happiest I'd ever been. Connor marched up to me not an hour later, demanding to know what kind of operation I planned to run because he was not letting it interfere with his lodge plans.

When I park in front of the main processing building, I'm shocked I'm still smiling, remembering the day I met Connor.

"What's got that smile on your face?" Sasha asks as he pulls off the helmet.

His hair pokes out all over from static and I reach for his hand. Pulling him along back to the sign we passed, I stop us in front and point to it.

"I came here with a dream. To own a sugar shack and make maple syrup. The best Canada would ever taste. I put that signpost in the ground before I even built my cabin." I chuckle again. "And not more than an hour later, Connor rolled up here and chewed me out for not keeping his family informed. He was still building the lodge, and it wasn't open. I had no business to inform about my plans, so that didn't happen."

"He thought you were pulling a fast one or something? Undercutting his business?"

"Nah. He didn't want someone bringing massive amounts of traffic here. He wanted a quiet road, and he was worried I might create a problem."

"So, how did you go from fighting with each other to getting married?"

Taking his hand, we walk back up to the buildings. The smile on my face is the biggest it's ever been since he died. With a laugh, I turn to Sasha.

"It wasn't overnight, but he had a crush after that meeting and he kept making excuses to drop by and ask how things were going. Before long, he was bringing me food, and we were sharing meals here. Then he was helping me and then... well, then we both realized we really liked each other. The rest is history, as they say."

Sasha smiles along with me and gets his camera out of the bag.

"It sounds like a great story. Maybe you'll share more with me?"

"Definitely. But what I want to show you is what I own here and why I wanted it so bad."

Sasha follows me along the path through the maple trees I used to tap. The equipment, if it's still any good, remains stored in the processing building and the path we walk is still slightly overgrown. Okay, lots overgrown. I should have warned him to wear pants just in case. Ticks and the other bugs out here can be a real annoyance.

But he doesn't seem to care, and he's fascinated with things I don't even look twice at. The fungus off a tree, a group of buttercups, and a tiny tree frog he spots near a patch off the trail.

"Look how cute it is, Leaf! I didn't know they made them that small." He leans in to photograph it and it jumps. He screeches, then bursts into laughter. "Oh my god, it scared the crap out of me!"

His innocent jubilation tugs me in like a magnet. My heart is light, and as we walk along this path, I show him where and how trees are tapped in the spring. As the time passes and he soaks it all in like a sponge, a hope grows. Hope that I enjoy living again.

Perhaps hope that I can also love again.

"How many trees are here, Leaf? You can't have tapped them all."

"I've lost track, but no, I didn't tap them all. But I had tapped 200 at one time. That's as big as I got. Then we decided to concentrate on the lodge since it was the bigger income generator and the plan was to work on this more in the winter."

Sasha pauses, sensing there's more to the story. And perhaps feeling the shift like I am. That there's once again hope for both of us.

"I'm getting thirsty. Do you mind if we head back for a break?"

"That's a good idea. You need to keep hydrated and I should have brought a water bottle with us. I wouldn't mind a drink myself."

Hand in hand, we silently walk the same way we came from, and the lightness I felt earlier remains.

Sasha isn't just beautiful.

He's smart and funny. Intuitive and incredibly strong.

And he's someone I like to spend time with.

Back at the cabin, I root the key from my pocket and force the door open. Dust streams through the beams of light, and the hot, stale air smacks into us.

"It's empty now and I don't know if the water even works out here anymore. I've neglected it."

The two-room cabin was my home for two years while I cleared timber and had the processing barn built. It was two years of immersing myself into everything maple syrup and somewhere in that busy part of my life, I allowed myself to fall in love with Connor.

He was unexpected. Much like Sasha.

Connor came here so often it wasn't until a year after meeting for lunch almost daily that he blatantly asked me if there was a reason I hadn't made a move on him yet. It shocked me so much to know someone like him was even attracted to me. But I kissed him that day. Right in this very room.

Oblivious to my memories, Sasha peeks into the tiny bathroom and back at me.

"Were you ever cold living here? It seems like you'd be cold."

"That's what the woodstove is for." I tap the iron stove near the back wall. "It made sense to use wood to heat the place. I'm surrounded by it and I had a bunch of trees to burn."

His lips fight a smile. "Did you chop the wood yourself, too?"

"Of course I did."

"Can you teach me how to chop a piece of wood?"

"I can, but it's not as easy as it looks."

He nods, accepting my information, and that determination of his that forces him to try different things never waivers.

"I want to try. When I came here, part of my goal was to try things people didn't think I'd be capable of." He hugs his arms around his waist. "People make a lot of assumptions about me and sometimes doing things to contradict those assumptions makes me...I don't know, feel validated in a way."

His honesty touches me. I don't think he knows how brave he actually is.

"Then let's get you chopping wood. I should still have axes over in the processing barn."

I explain as we lock the cabin and walk to the barn that it was a joint decision between Connor and me to stop working the sugar bush until we got the lodge running efficiently and could give it the time it needed. All the taps and tubing, bottles and pails and whatever else were stored here, collecting dust.

The time to reopen it never came because Connor died. There was no room in my life to return here and take it on. Especially when it held so many memories.

More dust greets us in the processing barn, and Sasha gasps.

"Holy crap! Is that a giant stove?"

Laughing, I pat my hand on the enormous wood fuelled processing stove.

"It is. The best way to process sap is by wood fire. You need a high temperature that a normal stove top just can't reach, so this baby burns hot. The sap goes in a giant vat up there. We monitor the sugar content and once it's at the right concentration, it funnels over here to cool and then get bottled."

"Wow." Sasha breathes and steps closer. He takes in the old setup with fresh eyes and his fascination reminds me of myself when I first learned all this stuff. And it ignites my want to do it again.

Locating my two favourite axes, I motion towards the door.

"Come on, let's get you learning to chop wood."

A pile of old wood sits in the centre of the main yard. Some of it has started to rot and might not even be good enough for a bonfire. But there're still some old pieces of oak and poplar that look up to the task of being chopped.

Hefting a large hunk of poplar on the chopping block, I explain to Sasha how the weight of the axe does most of the work for you. I demonstrate with a few swings into the block of wood and when I turn back to Sasha, his cheeks are flushed a gorgeous pink. Even his neck.

"Are you okay? You look flushed? Do you need water?"

Setting the axe against the wood block, I stride towards him. My heart races with thoughts of him being sick or heat stroked. I should have made him drink more.

"N-no. I'm good. Very good. You, ah... *hoo*... I was not aware watching a lumberjack in action would be this hot."

"So you're not sick?"

He shakes his head slowly and lightly bites at his lip.

"Oh, no. Nope. Not sick. Hot though. Very hot. The good kind."

Now it's my turn to be uncomfortable as Sasha looks at me like I'm his next meal. And I don't hate it.

"So, do you still want to learn how to do it?" My lips twitch as I try not to smile. "Or are you too overheated?"

His gorgeous lips tilt into a smile that's pure sex, and my pulse races.

"A hundred percent, yes, I still want to do *it*." Sasha draws out the *t* and licks his lips. His eyes sparkle with mischief and I draw a breath to steady myself.

He places his camera on the ground, nestling it on top of his bag a safe distance away. Once he's beside me, I have him get used to the weight of the axe in this hand.

"Now what you need to be prepared for is if the blade doesn't go through the wood, the axe bounces back. You need to control that and be prepared." Stepping away, I position my feet and instruct him on how to brace his lower body.

"That's your speed lesson to chop wood. Are you ready?"

He nods and takes a few steadying breaths. Then he raises the axe over his head with great form—just like I showed him—and swings down to the wood. The axe bounces as I suspected it would, and he yelps while taking a step back.

"Jesus, that hurts. Oh. My. God." He sets the axe down gingerly and grabs at his shoulder.

"Damn it. I'm sorry. I forgot to tell you—the vibrations can be uncomfortable." I push his hand away and massage his shoulder and arm. "You're okay? Do you want to keep going?"

"Yes. I said I'd do this and I will."

He shakes me off and picks up the axe again. Bracing his feet and steadying himself again, he swings. It bounces back, and he sets his jaw before repositioning. The muscles in his arms pop and he swings a third time. This time the blade sticks, and he whoops with joy.

"I'm doing it, Leaf!"

"You are! Keep going!"

Sasha doesn't have great arm strength, and he's already strained to his max by the way his muscles tremble when he finally frees the axe from the wood. A day in the gym has nothing on the workout chopping wood can be. But he pauses to wipe the sweat from his brow and continues on.

Finally, his swing goes through the piece of wood and it splits. He steps back, shaking and sweating, but with a smile so big I can't help myself.

I swoop him in my arms and hug him so tight he grunts with the pressure.

"You did it, baby! I'm so proud of you!" And I kiss him. Without thinking, I press my lips to his, so filled with his joy at accomplishing his goal.

And he's kissing me back.

I want to tell him everything I'm feeling and try to explain what today has meant to me, but only his name crosses my lips. Breathless and wanting more, I don't know how to say it.

Instead, he slides his hands into my short beard and says, "Me too, Leaf. Me too."

Chapter 11
Sasha

Who knew chopping wood could be such an aphrodisiac?

Watching Leaf power his way through blocks of wood like they were butter was incredibly erotic. Maybe it was the way his broad back stretched under his shirt or the way he made this little puff of air every time the axe met the wood. Whatever it was, it captured my attention like nothing else ever has.

And the kiss?

I've never in my life been kissed like that. It started with joy that I'd accomplished yet another task I'd never thought I could do, but quickly morphed into more. The passion in Leaf burst forth unlike any of our other encounters. It was there on his lips and his touch and the way he breathed my name.

I wanted to shout to all the creatures in this forest how amazing it was. I also wanted to rip all his damn clothes off and beg him to do wicked things to me that might involve an accidental splinter in my ass.

But none of that happened because the rumble of another ATV came up the path and Leaf's brother, Perry, came into view.

"Ah, I hoped I'd find you here."

He kills the engine and removes his helmet, running a hand through his hair. The puff of exhaust lingers and as fun as riding in these things are, I can't say I'm a fan of all the dust and exhaust smells.

"Hey, Perry." Leaf calls and I wave to be polite. Our first encounter left a mixed taste in my mouth, but he's Leaf's brother, so I don't want to be rude.

"Everything okay here?"

Perry glances my way as he and Leaf exchange a silent conversation.

"Everything is fantastic. Right, Sasha?"

Leaf snakes his arm around my waist and smiles down at me. It's an automatic response to smile back and I hug his waist, too.

"Definitely fantastic. Completely enlightening and perhaps a bit... eye opening."

Leaf swallows, and his tongue darts out to lick his lips. Yeah, we're on the same page with things.

"Good. Listen, I wanted to invite you two out tonight. It's been ages since we've gone to the bar, Leaf. It's wing night at the Log Jam tonight and I think Sasha might like to see more of what this town offers other than great coffee and a bookshop."

Has he been spying on me? Even if he did, a night on the town with Leaf sounds like something I'd never turn down. Watching him in his element is great, but I'd like to see Leaf out of it too. It seems only fair to me. Although once again I'll be at a disadvantage.

"I'd love to! That sounds really fun. What's a wing night?"

Both Leaf and Perry stare at me, incredulous, trying to assess if I'm pulling their leg. But I truly don't know what a wing night is.

"Wing. Night." Perry says slowly. "It's a night. For wings. Chicken wings?"

"Please tell me you've had chicken wings before." Leaf says and I feel my neck heat.

"Uh...no. I've ah... I wasn't allowed to eat a lot of things when I was still under contract. I lived on vegetables, hummus, and lean chicken. Not much else. But I want to try a chicken wing!"

And I really do. I'm not sure why, but it feels like one of those things I might have done with friends if I hadn't been so sheltered.

"Wow. You really are here to do all the things." Leaf's fingers flex on my hip and when I meet his eyes, there's a new look there. It's curious and I squeeze back.

"All the things. Yep."

Perry clears his throat.

"So, it's best to get there early since it gets so busy. We can take one vehicle and I'll ask Millie to have a summer student stay late to help with after supper duties if that's okay?"

Leaf nods slowly, and he eases his arm around my waist. His hand rests on the small of my back while his thumb smoothes small circles through my shirt.

"Why don't you take your own vehicle and we'll take my truck? You'll want to go home after and you live in town. No sense driving us home and back. The lodge is full, so you can't crash in an empty room."

Perry considers this with a sigh. "Right. Two trucks then. I'll head back now and make sure it's all arranged." He places his helmet back on and makes it a point to only address Leaf. "It's been a long time, brother. I'm looking forward to it."

He fires up his ATV and rolls away with a wave, leaving us alone again and watching the dust kick up behind him.

"Are you sure you want to go to a bar in this tiny town and try chicken wings?"

"A hundred percent."

"What about drinking beer?"

I wrinkle my nose. "I'm not a fan. How about rye?"

He nods in approval. "I can work with that. What about dancing? Do you dance?"

Now it's my turn to stare in disbelief. "Do I dance? Leaf, if I wasn't a model, I'd be a dancer. This body has moves, so it's best you be prepared."

He smiles again, and the crinkles by his eyes deepen. Leaning down, he places a kiss on my forehead. "Something tells me I'll never be prepared when it concerns you."

"You ain't seen nothing yet." I wink, and instead of a laugh I was hoping for, he cocks his head. Those deep, thoughtful eyes see all the way into my deepest, darkest secrets.

"Then I look forward to what you still have to show me."

Leaf locked up the buildings and returned me to my cabin. It wasn't his original plan for the day. He wanted us to have dinner in his suite and while I would have loved the quiet alone time, I'm also curious about the town.

I didn't come here hell-bent to eat a chicken wing, but either way, I'm excited to be on a date with Leaf. And it's a public one. I feel like that might be a bigger step for him than me at this point. But I'll take it.

I'm not sure what kind of dress is acceptable here so I keep it low-key. A pair of skinny jeans and a gorgeous, pale pink t-shirt in the softest of cottons. Rooting through my jewellery tote, I dress it up with a low-hanging gold chain and my favourite pink coral ring that I bought on a shoot we did in Cuba once. Sure, it's just a costume piece, and sometimes the silver tarnishes while I wear it, but it's just so damn pretty.

Styling my hair in a casual mess, I add the pink lip gloss Leaf liked before and just a hint of mascara. Being outside so much the past few weeks has allowed the sun to colour my face and I look healthy. Gone is the paleness of a sick Elizabethan child. I look invigorated. Alive and ready to take on the world. Perhaps more confident in this version of me than ever before.

A light knock on the door sends the butterflies into a flurry in the pit of my stomach and I run to open it.

Leaf stands there, so handsome it knocks the breath out of me. He's ditched the plaid and wears a simple red t-shirt with a less-worn pair of jeans. His neatly trimmed beard looks extra soft. His hair still flops over his forehead like a young boy's and my heart thumps, all wacky.

"Wow, you're gorgeous."

He blurts and both of us laugh at his unexpected outburst.

"I think I just said the quiet part loud. That was supposed to stay in my head."

Still laughing, I step out of the cabin and rest a hand on his chest.

"For what it's worth, I thought the same thing about you."

"Thank you." Under that beard I know he's blushing, and it makes my heart melt. He takes my hand as we walk to his truck and he explains to me the relationship with his brother.

"I know Perry was harsh with you the first time you met, but he's a good guy. He's my little brother, and he moved here when I told him I wasn't leaving."

"You're close then."

He nods. "Very. He used to join Connor and me at these nights out. I want you to know that these outings mean a lot to him."

A prickle of unease crosses my skin.

"Is this... I know he invited me, but is this okay? I feel like I'm suddenly in a position that I won't be able to fill."

If Perry wants to have what he used to with his brother-in-law, I'm not sure I'll ever live up to those expectations.

Leaf stops and turns me towards him. The fading sunlight is enough for me to notice the furrow of his brow. His concern that I misunderstood.

"No one is comparing you, Sasha. I don't want you to feel like that. I just want you to know that Perry cares for my happiness. He's a bit of a meddler and he's sometimes ultra annoying, but he's so full of love. He'll kill me for telling you that, but he has a lot of layers if you're patient."

Nodding, I squeeze his hand. "Thank you. I won't tell, and that does make me feel better."

Leaf kisses my cheek and helps me into his truck like a true gentleman. Not that I need help, but he's treating this like a real date. A new start. Even though I kind of like what we've already experienced together, the date is a next level.

"All buckled?"

He beams over at me and my stomach goes all flippy again.

"Yep."

"Are you ready for chicken wings?"

"As long as I don't have to pluck feathers off them... yes!"

Leaf booms a laugh and winks.

"Not this time, anyway."

They don't really do that. He's joking. Right?

The Log Jam is a restaurant and bar that is just as adorable as the rest of the town. The sign out front has a man with a giant pole and spiked boots standing on a raft. Or maybe it's logs? I'll have to ask later because once we're inside, it's like a record scratch in my brain.

The ratio of plaid and beards to clean shaven in t-shirts is about 40 to 1. If you have a lumberjack fetish, beard kink, or hell, any kind of lust for the manly mountain-type guys, you need to come here and have your mind blown.

I need to sneak photos for Roman. This is too much.

"Let's grab that table over there by the bear." Leaf's hand on my back steers me towards a wooden bear statue and I laugh.

"Will you take my picture with that bear?"

"Uh, sure."

I hand Leaf my phone and ham it up as if the bear was attacking me and another photo with me hugging it.

"Roman—he's my best friend back home—he teased me about getting attacked by a bear while I was here. He'll get a kick out of that."

Leaf laughs and hands my phone back as we slide into the booth.

"He sounds fun. But remind me to make sure you know how to use bear spray if you hike by yourself."

What!?

Leaf closes his hand over mine. "There's nothing to worry about. Except what flavour of wings you want to try."

"Good evening... oh my gosh! Leaf! It's so wonderful to see you!"

He stands to hug the waitress, who barely looks old enough to serve alcohol, and when she glances at me, we both do a double take. It's the girl from the park I met.

"Violet, right?"

"You two know each other?" Leaf furrows his brow, looking between us.

"We met at the park the other day. He gave me his autograph. How do you find yourself friends with this amazing human, Leaf? Not that you're not amazing yourself, but you know who he is, right?"

Leaf glances at me, and I shrug.

"Uh, Sasha. He's a model—"

"Former model I'd say." I smile as Leaf continues to look confused.

"He's an example is what he is. He did a spread a few months ago in a magazine that was so inspiring. Sasha gave a lot of us hope for good things and to always be ourselves." She winks at me. "He's not just a pretty face, Leaf."

Leaf squirms and seems uncomfortable, but he smiles at Violet.

"I know."

She falls into the spiel of wing night specials and leaves a menu. Violet even asks if Perry will join us, which makes me wonder what the connection is. I know it's a small town, but Violet is so young.

"Hi guys, sorry I'm late."

Perry slides into the booth next to me with a smile.

"Did you order yet?"

"No, Leaf was just explaining all the choices."

"Violet already met him at the park." Leaf throws out. "She knows who Sasha is."

Perry turns to me. "No shit. You're already meeting people here." He glances at Leaf. "Did you tell him who Violet is?"

Leaf's eyes lose a little shine and he bites his lip.

"Don't tell me if you don't want to."

"I want to. It's just—"

The young lady herself appears again and interrupts to take our orders. Leaf and Perry are determined for me to try a dill pickle flavoured chicken wing. I agree but only with honey garlic as a backup because I know I'd like that. Who eats pickle-flavoured chicken?

Only once she's returned with our drinks and my glass of rye and ginger ale is in front of me, does Leaf pick up the conversation.

Both he and Perry sip from tall glasses of beer and I smile when some of the foam sticks on Perry's mustache.

"Okay, so Violet is a great kid. I've known her since I moved here. She used to come to the lodge all the time." He takes a breath. Another. "She's Connor's best friend's daughter. She's like a niece."

When Leaf pauses to drink his beer, I notice the small shake of his hand.

"Violet was in the car with Connor when he died." Perry says, voice low. "She carries guilt. She was only twelve, but she thinks if she knew first aid she could have helped him. She stopped coming to the lodge with her dad because she thought Leaf hated her."

My heart breaks for both Violet and Leaf. How awful for her, such a young child, to go through such an experience. Leaf lost more than just Connor that day. Even though Violet welcomed him here tonight, there must still be a rift in their relationship.

"Leaf... I'm so sorry."

"Everyone is." He shrugs and looks away, and I glance at Perry. He signals it's okay and to just wait, so I sip my drink while all I want to do is hug the man across from me so hard that all his broken pieces smoosh back together.

Leaf jumps back into the conversation as if nothing happened and the lovable lumberjack returns.

"So, what do you think of this place? I bet you don't find this in the city."

I snort at the massive understatement.

"I can't say I have. It's unique, I'll give you that." Glancing to my left, I notice a few burly looking men watching us closely and I quickly turn back to face Leaf.

"Do I stand out too much? Those men are staring."

Old Sasha would smile and flirt and try to keep their attention all night. But current Sasha wants to be just another person here and not singled out. Unless it's by the man seated across from him.

"You'll stand out whether you want to or not, baby. Don't mind them. Unless you're uncomfortable?"

Leaf's use of an endearment here freezes me in place. He doesn't seem to care that he said it and he casually looks their way.

"Let them look, I say." Perry bumps my shoulder. "They're just a couple of guys in a bar looking around. Pay no attention."

Maybe they're right and I'm overreacting.

I want to apologize for my insecurities and to assure them both I'm not a self-centred asshole, but Leaf chooses the moment I open my mouth to slide his hand across the table and squeeze mine. His warm brown eyes shine.

No apology is needed. He fucking knows. Just like everything else he learns about me, he doesn't need my words to confirm it.

I want to ask him how he does that, but Violet chooses that moment to show up with enough wings to feed a small army. Leaf's laughter at my reaction to the mountain of chicken wings is worth being stared at a second time.

"Before you ask, yes, we'll eat them all. Perry and I love chicken wings. The Log Jam makes them the best."

Perry chooses a few wings and places them on a plate for me. He points to each one and explains.

"Dill pickle and Salt and Pepper are the dry ones. Honey garlic and Maple BBQ are the sauce ones. The brown one is honey garlic. Nothing spicy. One is a wing and one is the drumette. Wings are harder to eat since the meat is between two bones, see?" He bites a wing and shows me the centre. "You get that out just with your tongue or teeth or whatnot. Some people break the bones away. And your fingers will get messy if you love the saucy ones like me."

Across from me, Leaf grins as I digest all of Perry's chicken wing eating tips. Who knew eating could be so challenging?

"Fuck, I've missed this," Perry says, and I'm not stupid. He's not talking about wings. He's smiling at his brother with a misty eye and now I get what Leaf meant when he said Perry had layers to him.

"Should I take a photo of this for you, Sasha?" Leaf teases.

And the twinkle of fun in his eyes as he laughs with his brother and nudges my foot under the table causes me to reach for my drink.

If I have a few drinks, I can blame all the emotions bubbling over on the alcohol.

Definitely not because I'm possibly falling in love.

Chapter 12
Leaf

Being at the Log Jam with Perry and Sasha was difficult at first. Too many memories of nights with Perry and Connor here kept coming back, and the old game of juggling grief and happiness kept poking in when it wasn't welcome.

But watching Sasha eat chicken wings for the first time is easily a highlight of my life. Babies get excited with new food and it's cute. Sasha gets excited with a new food and he's planning how to own his own restaurant so he can have chicken wings every day.

And the dill pickle flavour he turned a nose up at? He loves it.

Perry excused himself after we had a few drinks and called himself a taxi home. Sasha and I linger a little longer before I finally make a move to get the night moving.

"Are you up for a walk before we go home?"

He pats his belly. "With the amount of food I've consumed tonight, yes. I should walk some of this off."

As I go to wave down Violet for the bill, Sasha pulls out his wallet.

"You're not paying. This is a date I asked you on."

His mouth moves, but no words come out. I motion to Violet that I'm ready to settle the tab.

"I hope you enjoyed yourself. There were a lot of laughs coming from this table tonight." Violet smiles warmly when she passes me the payment machine.

Tapping my card to pay, I nod and smile back while waiting for the song of an approved payment.

"It was a great night." Pausing, I look up at the young girl, who's now a young woman, with great fondness. "It was great to see you, Violet. I miss you."

And I really do. I avoided her because she couldn't erase the guilt over Connor. Any time she came over after he died, it was like she was afraid to speak and it was too painful for me. I had to grieve for my husband and I didn't have it in me to set her heart at ease then.

She blinks rapidly and nods. "Thanks. I miss you, too. It's great to see you out again."

"It's good to be out." Swallowing hard, I take her hand in mine. "Listen, come by the lodge before you go off to school in the fall? I don't want to miss you before you go."

"Can we fish off the dock this summer?" her voice cracks and I swallow back the lump in my throat. I still see her with her pigtails laughing as we fished for hours, catching perch that fit in the palm of your hand.

"Let me know when and I'll make it happen, Vi."

Standing quickly, I take her in my arms and she clutches me tight.

"I'm sorry I let you drift away." I whisper into her hair. "You're my family. I love you and I'd love to catch up soon."

When she lets me go, her cheeks are wet and I wipe them away. She smiles, though, and nods. "I'll hold you to it."

She again greets Sasha and tells us how happy we look and when she's called away to another table, I feel like I'm both empty and full as she walks away.

"You ready, beautiful?"

Holding my hand out to Sasha, he smiles shyly, almost in disbelief that I'd offer my hand to help him from the booth. He says nothing about my exchange with Violet either, which I appreciate.

"Born ready."

Into the warm night air, we stroll down the main street of Maple. Clasping his hand in mine feels perfect. So perfect I feel the squeeze in my chest when I think of how many days he has left here. There's so much I want to show him and teach him.

But first, I owe him some background.

"Oh, the park looks so pretty at night." Sasha beams at me. "This is where I met Violet and her friends."

"Which end of the park did you come in on?"

He motions to the other side, which makes sense since it's closer to where Pete would pick up and drop him off.

"I'd like to tell you more about Connor, if you don't mind."

He squeezes my hand. "I'd love to know more about him. Whatever you want to share."

Walking down the path to the entrance of the park, I tell him how Connor grew up here and even though he had a dream of running a lodge on his family's property, he had a degree as an arborist.

"Wait, so Connor had an issue with you cutting trees on your property? Is that what really got him to stop at your sugar bush?"

Chuckling, I shake my head. "Not at all. But the funny thing is, if you want to get technical, he's the one who was a real lumberjack. He had a degree specializing in trees. It doesn't get more lumberjack than that."

"That's so funny." Sasha laughs softly and, as we approach the park sign I've avoided since it went up, I'm shocked I'm still smiling.

"His passion was urban planning, and he had two summer placements with the town while he was in university. He convinced them to turn this very space into a park. Just to preserve some of the woods in town and not let it get gobbled up by buildings."

Sasha nods along in agreement.

"It's a great place. The first day I came to town, I saw the park from the bridge. I stopped to watch the ducks because it reminded me of my mom. I came back here after..." he clears his throat. "After you spent the night to talk it over with

Roman. I needed to clear my head, and the ducks came and... well, I was mostly at ease here."

When we get to the sign, my eyes burn, but my smile is still in place.

Connor Sweet Memorial Park
We dedicate this park to Connor Sweet.
A Maple resident who wanted everyone to slow down and enjoy life to the fullest.
Gone too soon, but never forgotten.

"He was alive when the park was built. It just didn't have a name. It was Violet's dad who brought the motion to the town council. They agreed, and he and I watched the day they erected the sign. On that day, I wasn't able to feel anything about the dedication. Grief was all I knew for so long. A few years ago, I came here by myself one night and it was better."

A single tear runs down my face, and I startle when Sasha reaches up to wipe it away.

"And now?" he murmurs.

"Now I'm so damn proud I was his husband. He was one of those people that everyone loved and lit up a room. He made you happy. He made *me* happy. I spent too much time being angry that he was taken from me and not enough time appreciating how fortunate I was to have had him in my life for as long as I did. I'm so proud of this place he created. He'll be a part of this town forever, just like he always wanted."

Sasha is silent, and I sneak a glance at him. He's such a beautiful person, inside and out. I don't want him to feel like

I'm comparing him to Connor, but I had to tell him and show him this. I owed it to him, because if Sasha wants to make something happen with us, Connor would always exist.

"My mom was a flighty, artist-type." His voice is soft as he leans into my side. "We moved from town to town a lot. She homeschooled me for most of my life. Since she was so free spirited, she often took me to a park where she painted and watched over me doing my homework." He smiles up at me, but his eyes are sad. "It had ducks. Feeding the ducks with my mom is something I miss. I came here when I saw them. It made me happy to watch the ducks." He huffs a small laugh. "Maybe it was fate. Two beautiful souls giving us both a place to find peace."

Running my fingers over the sign with a whispered good night, I tug him over to the bench nearby to watch the small creek running through town. It's nothing spectacular, but it brings the ducks he loves and kids like to catch frogs and watch for turtles here. He leans his head on my shoulder, and I wrap an arm around him. The moon reflects on the water and occasionally we hear the hum of a car's motor or the muted voices of pedestrians on their way home, but it might as well just be the two of us out here.

Sasha's hand rests on my knee and the ache to have him stay with me here, to not leave when his time is up, is so strong I have to bite my lip.

"Have you wondered if karma sometimes does bad things to help good people?" His voice is so small I have to strain to hear.

"What do you mean?"

"I wouldn't have come here if I hadn't broken my arm last year, finally got the courage to speak out against someone I trusted who was taking advantage of me, and I got fired. If any of that had not happened, I'd still be flirting with anyone that smiled at me and partying all the time. I'd still be waking up with people whose name I don't know and forgetting my mother left me in the care of someone who abused their privilege." He shifts on the bench and peers up into my eyes.

"If Connor hadn't died, you'd not have visited me with a bottle of wine or kissed me. Yet here we are, two broken people maybe figuring things out together. In another time, our paths would never have crossed."

"You're right. We'd never have met."

"I only have a week left."

"I know."

"I don't know what to do, Leaf."

His words take my breath away. Is he thinking about staying? Do I try to convince him? Fuck.

"I don't know either Sasha."

He places his hand on my cheek and his eyes swim with so many emotions. I'm only just pulling myself out of the same confusing pool of conflict, but one thing has been on my mind since this morning.

"Would you still like to see my place?" laughing softly, I take his hand to my lips. "I want you to see where I live in the lodge and what I call home."

Sasha leans up and kisses me on the cheek so tenderly I fear he might say no.

"I would love to. Does it come with breakfast?"

My heart stutters and trips as he bites his pink lip and I take a huge leap. Trusting that these past few weeks haven't been in vain and I'm ready to live a life again.

"I'll even serve it to you in bed."

His smile is sweet and shy. "Then I accept and request pancakes with that delicious syrup you make."

I pull him to his feet and together we weave our way through the park and back to my truck at the Log Jam. There's so much we need to work out and say and yet... do I tell him what I feel with him only here for a short while?

For the first time since Connor died, I'm ready to take my life back. And I'd like to do it with Sasha.

But do I risk breaking my heart again?

Chapter 13
Sasha

L eaf has been nothing short of incredible tonight. He brought me to a bar where I know I stood out like the spaghetti stain on your white shirt, but Leaf didn't bat an eye. He laughed with me, not at me, when I snatched up chicken wings like they were the last meal of my life.

And he called me baby in front of his brother. I don't think I'll ever get that out of my head. A single word has never made me feel so special. So cherished when it's given by Leaf.

But learning about Violet's connection to him and hearing about Connor and the park named after him was by far the most intimate of details Leaf could share. It's been overwhelming, but the picture of the man Leaf really is has become clearer. It's a picture I fear I may like too much.

My knee bounces as he parks in his space on the other side of the lodge. It's not the main lot where I was dropped off here in a clunky school bus what feels like forever ago.

"I thought the bit of worn grass was a path for deliveries or something." Glancing out the truck window, there's a tiny deck and railing with a light on above a very home-like door. A single railing planter filled with pink wave petunias spills over and makes me smile. It's a hint at the soft side of Leaf.

"Did you plant those?"

His teeth flash in the darkness of the truck cab, and his small chuckle sets my heart pounding.

"Every year. I choose a different colour every spring, though, to change it up. Those are called Pink Ladies. Pretty, right?"

His soft gaze finds mine and I know he doesn't just mean the flowers.

"Yes, they are. Pretty and resilient."

He tips his head in agreement and I break his gaze, finding the door handle so I can step out and take a breath.

We meet on his porch step and he absently plucks a few dead blooms from the flowers. I shouldn't be so enthralled with the way he tends to a planter of flowers, but I am. Everything Leaf does is with care and concern, and this is no different.

"You should see the view from upstairs. It's breathtaking."

"I'd love to."

Although the view in front of me is already breathtaking, I'm curious to see where Leaf calls home.

He holds the door open and I step inside to a small landing where coats hang on hooks across the wall and footwear collects on mats. A small wooden bench sits tucked in the corner and I wonder if Leaf made it. A short stairwell leads up to his space and after leaving our shoes in the entranceway, I follow him up.

The stairs end in his main living area and I immediately drift to the entire wall of windows looking out to the lake. His living area and kitchen are open concept, but this is the focal point. He arranged a sitting area at one end of the windows and I point to the love seat there.

"Is this facing east or west?"

He grins. "East. I love watching the sunrise."

"This is an amazing space, Leaf. It's so... calming and peaceful."

"Thank you. We're at the back of the lodge above the kitchen. The door over there leads down directly to the kitchen. I rarely use the door we came in on." He points into the darkness at the end of the windows. "The hallway leads to the bedroom and bathroom. It's cozy and I love it here."

His lips tilt in a half smile, like he's a little embarrassed to say that out loud.

"I can see why. It's like another world here, away from the rest of the lodge."

"It provides privacy when I need a day off, but I'm still close by if needed." He opens a small fridge under the kitchen island. "Would you like a drink? Wine or water? Maybe tea?"

"No, thanks."

We stand there awkwardly, both of us fidgeting with our hands, and I step over to him. With my heart in my throat, I channel the bravery I've been working hard on over the past few weeks.

"Now that I'm here, are you okay with me in this space?"

He's shared so much with me and we've been intimate in my cabin, but this is a big deal. I know he invited me, but I need to know.

His lips waver with a sigh laced heavy with nerves. "Yes. You look good here."

Three days ago, I wished I knew where his door was so I could go to him. Now I know where to find him and I'm in the space Leaf calls home. The handmade quilts placed over the backs of furniture, the reading glasses left on the table near his sunrise loveseat and the candle that he must have burned recently because the scent of orange blossom still hangs in the air. All those small things cement the realness of where I am.

Part of me wants to turn around and walk away. To protect my heart from attaching itself to him further, but I can't. The part of me that wants to experience all of Leaf, to have those same hands that so tenderly plucked at his flowers on me, is one I can't ignore. I might regret it later, but I'll deal with it then.

For now, I'm going to live and experience what it feels like to be cherished by this man.

"Sasha?"

Leaf's concerned voice pulls me from my drifting thoughts and I return my attention to the warm eyes of a man who's never far from my thoughts.

"I always wondered if guys with beards conditioned them." I blurt and he snort laughs. "I mean until I felt your beard, I thought it would be coarse. But it's not."

"Are you asking for beauty tips, Sasha?"

"Well, I don't have a beard. I'm just curious. Nervous and curious."

His brows knit, and he reaches for me.

"Why are you nervous?"

"I just... you're the first person I've ever let get this close to me. I've told you things that nobody but my best friend knows. And that makes me nervous." Swallowing, I brush my fingers through his short beard. "And I like you. That makes me extra nervous."

Nervous because I've given him the power to hurt me. I've never let my shield down for anyone like this before. Not since Moe manipulated me as a young boy into modelling, and acted more like a pimp than an agent, have I ever let anyone in like this. No one has ever had all of me. And a man I've known for a few short weeks has snuck in with a can opener and deftly opened all I've held so close to me. I'm now in a situation that is as foreign to me as wearing white after Labour Day.

"Oh, baby. We're in the same boat here. I told myself I never wanted to do this again. But you... you make me want it so much." His calloused hand cups my face. "You've made me smile without trying and for the first time in what feels like forever, I want to wake up with someone. Share my life again. Hell, eat chicken wings and laugh. I've missed out on so much. These past few weeks, you've made me realize how much I've missed living."

"Promise I get pancakes in the morning?" I whisper.

"Promise."

His lips brush mine, and I clutch at his shirt. Kissing him back, he moans deep and his beard tickles my cheek. "Let's do this right," he mumbles against my lips before gently tugging me down the short hallway.

The bedroom is almost as big as the main living area, but there's only one small window that opens and a beautiful set of French doors. Leaf follows my gaze.

"That leads to my little secret, and I'll show you later."

"Still mysterious. How charming."

My heart slams into my ribs and the tender look in Leaf's eyes sends a shiver through me. Is it possible he's just like the men in my favourite books? I've been brave, trying so many things while here, but letting someone get so close is more terrifying than the bear encounter Roman teased me about.

"I've never been called charming before. Mysterious, yes, but not charming."

Again, he places a hand on my cheek, and I bite my lip at the gentleness that resides in those hands. "But I'm honest, Sasha. And I meant what I said earlier. You woke me up. There's something about you I can't ignore." His lips kiss my forehead and he stays there with a shaky sigh. "Don't make me beg. If this is one-sided, tell me now."

"It's not one-sided." I whisper, and his body sags as he kisses my head again. "But you know if begging is a kink, we can work with it." I joke and a puff of air crosses my cheek as he laughs.

His hand trails down my side and his fingers dip under my shirt. The hairs of his beard dust over my skin and when I fist his shirt with my hands, he covers them with his own.

"Let me take care of you. I know you're scared and I am too, but I can lead us if it's easier for you."

I feel like an idiot, but I nod, and with gentle hands he removes my shirt, taking time to feather kisses across my chest and swirl his tongue across my nipples. My hands reach for his body and I tug his shirt over his head. His hair pokes up all crazy and I laugh softly.

"Did you use gel or mousse in your hair tonight?"

A blush sweeps up his neck. "Yeah. Why?"

Giggling, I smooth his wonky hair back. "You look like the guy in that movie who has cum in his hair and the woman thinks it's hair gel."

He kisses my knuckles, his gaze never wavering from mine.

We've already seen each other naked. We've shared orgasms and plenty of intimate touches, but this is different. It's not hurried or awkward and saturated with lust.

There's so much more crackling here and Leaf's lips on my skin snap me back to the present again. The reality of this broken man finding himself whole again with me is unexpected and I'm not prepared to handle all these new feelings that keep erupting.

"Stop thinking. Let's just be, Sasha. Let us just be. Right now. It's you and me. Even if it's just for tonight."

His fingers fumble with the buttons on my skinny jeans, and with a strained laugh, I help him.

"These are just as hard to get into as they are to get out of. Let me."

I shimmy and pull the tight pants off to Leaf's amusement.

"I have to say, I'm quite happy I don't follow fashion trends." He unzips and pushes his jeans over his hips and they slide to his knees. After stepping out of them with ease, he pulls me close to him again. "Getting undressed shouldn't leave you short of breath. It's what comes after that should take your breath away."

"Are you planning to take my breath away?"

Those damn brown eyes see into my deepest secrets, but I stand firm. He already found his way into everything, no sense trying to hide now.

"Just enough so you don't forget me."

And I fold into his strong arms. He's safe and kind and his touch is so... reverent. There's no mistaking that I'm not just a fling or a hot ass to use for a night. Leaf means every word, every kiss, and every touch. I can't turn him away, even if I wanted to. I'm too weak to avoid the broken heart that I know is on the horizon, but I'll bask in his worship for one night just so I know what it feels like to be someone's treasure.

He slides off my skimpy thong with care and a hum of approval before shedding his boxers, and I'm a panting puddle of desire. He backs me to the bed and lays me out more gently than I'd like, but it's exactly what I need.

Leaf's touch burns a path along my skin. Talented hands turn me into putty and my hips move on their own, seeking more. More touches, more kisses, more hot breath on my skin. His lips do nothing to quench the want, and before I know it, I'm the one begging.

"Please, Leaf..."

He gives me no words in reply, but instead fills me with another finger.

And dammit if I don't lose my breath for a moment.

"Leaf..."

My hands are talons, clawing at his head to pull his lips to mine. I can't seem to say anything other than his name and instead I pour my emotions into kisses. Frantic, passion-filled kisses I hope he understands.

He does, because his answer is gently shifting and reaching for a condom, which he places on my stomach.

"Can you put it on me?" He rasps and now is probably not the best time to tell him I've never done that before, either. My partners have always taken care of it, even if I asked. I just accepted that's how it is.

It's an unsexy, icky task for many people. Rushing past it if they can. But I don't see it that way and Leaf understands. Even if he doesn't know I've never placed one on another man, he just knows this is a big deal for me. To be trusted with it and still be in control. It's now my choice and this one tiny gesture knocks the last wobbly brick over around my heart.

Nodding, I take the package, tear it open, and sit up. Once I close my hand around the base of his cock, he drops his head to my shoulder with a moan.

Kissing his shoulder, I roll it on, pleased that I handled the pressure and didn't fuck it up. Still on our knees, he cradles my face and kisses me so sweetly it breaks my heart.

"Are you okay?"

"Yes, are you?"

Leaf blinks back at me. Surprised, I asked his own question. "I'm right where I want to be."

Smirking, finally feeling a tad like myself, I lay back down.

"I'm almost there. Once you join me, I'll be where I want to be."

And I should be elated when he settles over me and my body welcomes him inside. Leaf wraps me in his arms and holds me like I'm the most precious thing in the world. All the while whispering in my ear how beautiful, smart, and brave I am. With each thrust of his hips I lose myself in the moment of feeling like I'm somebody special, that I'm adored... that I'm maybe even loved even if he doesn't say the words.

And with that realization, I squeeze him tighter and bury my face in his neck.

Because I don't know how to love.

Even after we've both reached our release and he cleans me up, gathering me in his arms to sleep, I lay awake.

Learning to fish, chop wood, and read trail maps has been affirming. My confidence has soared. My mornings with books and walks on the beach have provided me ample time to reflect on my future and what path I'll take.

And until now, I thought I had it figured out.

But Leaf is an unexpected complication and I don't know what to do.

Chapter 14
Leaf

Leaving Sasha sleeping in my bed, I sneak out to the kitchen and brew a single cup of coffee. The sun isn't even close to rising yet, but I need time to collect my thoughts before I make the pancakes he bargained for.

Shifting against the cushions, I stare into the still black sky. One week left with Sasha and I won't even be able to spend it all with him.

With a sigh, I pick at the cushion. A gift from Millie after Connor died. A simple white canvas with the words, *"Love is everywhere"*. It was her way of reminding me that even though he's gone, he's still around.

Which he is.

I think of him and remember something we did or said every day. I don't cry myself to sleep or anything, but I miss him. He left a huge hole in my life. Sasha will never fill that hole. They're two completely different people, but damn, he makes me happy. I just wish he'd give me a little more of him.

His ex-agent, this Moe guy, hurt him and it breaks my heart to know Sasha is all alone. To know that Moe was supposed to protect him, but used him like he did. He gave me more last night when he opened up about his mother, but he's guarding himself. I can feel it every time he touches me.

Last night was a turning point. Sasha gave me his body and I know it wasn't a light decision. He says he trusts me, but I feel the fear he holds just a footstep away.

I understand because I've been in that same place since Connor died. Now that I've let that go and allowed myself to feel for someone, the best I can do is brace for Sasha's departure. I can't make him stay, even if there is a way to work it out.

"Hey."

Sasha stands before me in one of my too-big t-shirts. His hair is bed messed, and he's adorably sleepy.

"It's still early. You can sleep more."

"How come you're up so early?"

He sits next to me on the small loveseat and curls up with his head on my shoulder. I hug him close with my free arm.

"I'm an early bird, and I wanted time to think before I made the pancakes you asked for."

"What are you thinking about?"

His voice is soft as his finger traces the pattern on my sleep pants.

I don't answer right away because he likely has an idea. Sasha isn't stupid. Quite the opposite, and I won't insult him by brushing it off and not being honest.

"You, mostly. How much I like having you here and when I'll get to see you again."

His breath hitches, and he squeezes my leg.

He remains quiet and I won't force a conversation he doesn't want to have. Especially if it's something I don't want to hear.

"Why don't you go back to bed? I'll make you the pancakes you love with extra syrup."

My heart twists when he rises and places a kiss on my cheek.

"Maybe I should. It was a late night, after all." He gives me a small smile and shuffles back to the bedroom. Every other step has the t-shirt bouncing and I catch a glimpse of his ass. While it's a welcome sight and one I could get used to, I wish he would have stayed with me on the loveseat. We could watch the birth of a new day and start it with a kiss.

God, when did I get so damn emotional?

Draining my coffee, I set about mixing the homemade pancake recipe Millie gave to me years ago. Light and fluffy pancakes for the man who deserves the world on a platter will be ready before long. Before I cook the batter, I pull out some bananas and strawberries and chop them up, putting them into small bowls. He'll probably bypass them and concentrate on the syrup, but I want him to have a choice.

Before long, the kitchen fills with the aroma of cooked pancakes and warm maple syrup. Even my mouth waters. Plating the cakes for him, I place it all on a cookie sheet to carry to the bedroom with the fruit and syrup.

But when I open the door, he's not in bed.

"Sasha?"

The bathroom is empty, which means there's only one other place he could be unless he crawled under the bed to hide. I know he has a lot on his mind, but I don't think he'd avoid me that much.

Cracking open the door to my tiny balcony, I go from heart broke to heart full.

"You found my secret hideaway."

Still in my shirt, he's laying in my free-standing hammock, gazing up at the fading morning stars. With one hand behind his head, the t-shirt rides up and his cock is on full display. I could get used to this view. He shifts his head at the sound of my voice.

"It's gorgeous out here."

Privacy glass surrounds my patio and hammock. Even if people were out and about, you can't see anyone up here unless you fly a drone. Sasha either knows this or doesn't care about his provocative pose. He makes a welcome addition to my patio. Some nights I drop netting over myself while I gently sway and listen to the calls of loons while watching for shooting stars. The only thing that would make that better is having him like this in the hammock with me on those nights.

"I do some of my best relaxing out here."

"I bet. There's just something about hammocks, isn't there?"

"I like to think it's because you feel weightless. All those tiny ropes take your weight. If they can physically carry you, maybe they can work on carrying your troubles, too."

He hums under his breath and turns back to the sky.

"Breakfast is ready. Pancakes like you asked for."

A real smile plays on his lips, and my shoulders relax.

"And the man cooks. You're quite the package, aren't you, Leaf?"

He shifts and easily maneuvers out of the hammock. Walking toward me, the twinkle is back in his eyes, and he reaches up on his toes to kiss my cheek again.

"So are you, Sasha."

Before he can brush past me, I snake my arm around his waist and pull him closer.

"You deserve all the things, Sash." I whisper in his ear and kiss his temple. "Any man who knows you properly would know you deserve to be treated like a prince. I'll start with pancakes because I'm just a lowly lodge owner."

His laughter shakes his body against mine and I'm pleased I did that.

"You got me. Let me taste these pancakes and see if they're fit for royalty or not."

Holding the door, I let him pass and I don't miss the soft exclamation of joy under his breath when he sees what I've brought him.

"Leaf... this is amazing! I've never had breakfast in bed before! How do I do it?"

Laughing, I lift the tray so he can settle on the bed and set it back in front of him.

"Just like when you're out of bed? Use the utensils and eat. I won't even care if you spill on the sheets."

His smile could illuminate outer space as he inspects everything on the tray.

"Oh Em Gee, the syrup is warm!" He pours more than half of it on his pancakes and watches it soak into the small stack I made him. He's like a kid on Christmas morning.

"Why," he stuffs another bite of pancake in his mouth, "does this taste so much better here?"

Laughing, I pop a piece of fruit into my mouth. "Because that syrup was made right here. It doesn't get any better than that. No preservatives and processing and extra flavours that take away from the *actual* flavour."

We laugh and talk through mouthfuls of food. My heart is lighter than it's been in years and my face hurts from all the laughs. When he's all but licked his plate clean, he fidgets with the dishes on the tray.

"Leaf… I should let you get to your day."

"You don't have to rush out. You can even stay here in the hammock if you want to. It's great for reading."

A soft huff. "Yeah, probably is. I'll see you later?"

"I'll come over when my guided fishing is done. It will be late. After supper, for sure, if that's okay?"

"Of course." He slides out of bed and pulls on his clothes from last night. He hesitates while removing my shirt.

"Keep it, Sasha. I don't mind."

"It's silly, I know…"

"Nothing you ever do or say is silly to me."

He follows me to the kitchen and after placing the tray on the counter, he motions to the stairwell to my private entrance.

"I'll get my shoes and leave that way, Leaf. Thank you. For last night and breakfast. It was wonderful."

"I'd like for us to do it again."

A cloud over his sunny face makes my heart sink.

"Yeah. Have a good day on the water, Leaf."

Before he gets too far, I call out, "Wait."

He turns and I walk over to him. His eyes are wide as I lean down and kiss him. Once, twice, and I memorize the feel of his lips and the taste.

"Have a good day, Sasha."

In a blink he has his shoes on, and the door clicks behind with a soft thunk.

And I wonder if it's the last time I'll get to kiss him.

Chapter 15
Sasha

Digging my toes in the sand, I allow the cool lake water to lap over my feet. After spending my morning with a book, I needed to walk and think. I brought my camera and walked on the beach until it ran out and I reached rocks and forest.

I sat on the rocks in the sun for I don't know how long, but my mind was just as foggy as when I started the walk. But I got some amazing shots of an eagle flying and a cool close-up of a swallowtail butterfly on a rock. Those are things I don't see often in the city.

Even the noise here is calming.

All I've heard today is the odd boat motor and muted conversations of fishermen or kayakers over the water. Bird songs and squirrel trills. Waves slowly rolling up the sandy beach.

None of it can drown out the anxiety that simmers inside me.

The waves splash and lap as I consider a fully clothed dunk in the water. But cool lake water won't wash all this away.

"Why am I so messed up? This shouldn't scare me so much."

Of course, there's nobody around to answer and my words drift off into the summer air. This getaway was supposed to be easy. Simple even. Quiet time to spend thinking about my photography and a business plan. Read books and rest. Try out new nature stuff. Eat s'mores!

With a snort, I recall fishing with Leaf. I not only caught a fish, but I held it without a fuss. I even smoked a cigar after. God, we laughed so much that day.

Swallowing the lump in my throat, I walk along the shore toward my cottage.

Leaf cooking me breakfast this morning and the way he held me last night... it's not casual. No one has ever treated me like Leaf did. I don't know how to handle it. I should, it's just someone being good and kind. Being a thoughtful lover and genuinely concerned about my experience.

Being treasured is how I felt. There was no other descriptor I could come up with. Leaf made me feel like there was no one else he'd rather be with.

And I loved it. I loved feeling special, and while the anxiety gnaws at what it all means, I can't forget the feeling.

But Leaf is still mourning what he lost. Where do I fit here?

"You lost in your thoughts, Sasha?"

Gasping, I drop my shoes and fumble for my camera bag.

"You scared the shit out of me, Perry! What are you doing here?"

He rises from the chair as I climb the steps of the small porch.

"Looking for you."

"Okay... why?"

He shifts on his feet, glancing at the lake before returning to me.

"Can we talk?"

With a nod, I unlock the door for us. He stands while I drop my shoes and place my camera on the table. He remains quiet, and it irrationally irritates me. Having him hover like this in my space.

"Well, what is it, Perry? Are you here to tell me I'm no good for your brother? I should just leave and the sooner I do, the sooner he'll forget?"

Perry's mouth drops.

"No... I ...no! What the hell? Is that what you think? I know I was an ass the first time we met, but I thought we had fun last night? You did like being out with us last night, didn't you?"

His look turns guarded and I know I could be mean right now. I could crush them both and stick to keeping everyone but Roman out. But my question has genuinely hurt Perry and as much as I'm confused, I can't hurt them. Not like this.

"It was one of the best nights of my life." My voice wavers and I wish it wouldn't. "I mean that Perry. I had a great time. It's just..."

Trailing off, I don't know how to put it into words. This wasn't supposed to happen. I feel like a fish out of water.

Gasping and hoping to go back to the world I know well, but also hoping I can figure out how to live a new life somewhere else.

"Listen, I just wanted to come and tell you thank you."

"Thank me? For what?"

Perry drops his head back, swallowing before his gaze returns to mine. His pale blue eyes shimmer and I feel like an absolute dick for being so rude.

"When Connor died, I lost him *and* my brother. Leaf has never been the same. I expected him to be different, but I never thought he'd stay that way." He runs a hand over his face with a sigh. "My brother died too, and last night he was back. The three of us used to hang out like that all the time. Leaf was happy for the first time in years, Sasha. Genuinely happy. And I have my brother again. So I wanted to thank you."

Sinking onto the sofa, I hold my head in my hands.

"Perry," I croak. "Thank you for telling me, but I... I don't belong here."

His jaw sets, and he nods. A heaviness hangs in the air as he gathers his words.

"I don't say a lot of nice things, Sasha. I'm brash and in your face and I don't believe in love. And I interfere with my brother when needed. Usually against his wishes. I asked you to come with us last night because I noticed how he looked and spoke to you. I knew he took you fishing, and I knew he took you to the place he left the other half of his heart." With a large breath, he continues and I shrink back as his voice slices like tiny shards of glass. "If you think you don't belong here, I can't make you change your mind. So I won't bother to list the ways you *do* fit here."

He turns toward the door, storm clouds now over his previously smiling face.

"Maybe I was wrong about you after all."

Perry leaves without another word, and I remain in the silence of the cabin. My thoughts are too loud and I pace around, packing clothes and items I've left strewn about.

Maybe I can call a taxi and leave before Leaf comes tonight. Do they even drive out this far? Dammit. I might need to track down Pete.

But instead of searching for Pete, I sag back onto the sofa.

At what point do I stop running from the things that scare me the most?

The cabin is dark when I'm drawn from my sleep by a gentle, yet persistent knock on the cabin door.

I know it's Leaf.

But I curl back into a ball and ignore it until he goes away.

With a backpack loaded with my phone, laptop, and camera, I'm at the lodge close to the time Pete runs the shuttle into town. I'm dying for a coffee and one of Millie's homemade muffins, but I don't want to go inside.

"Hey, Sasha. We missed you at breakfast."

"Pete! Hi, I slept in. But I need to go to town. Are you going in?"

He nods slowly. "I am. I need to do some errands for Millie. I'm just about to get the list from her. Come on in with me."

"Oh, I'll just wait —"

"Come with me, son. We'll get the list and split."

Pete leaves no room to argue and I follow him inside to the kitchen, where Millie laughs with the kitchen staff as she writes on a whiteboard.

When she sees me, the smile that splits her face is hard not to return.

"Sasha, love! We missed you at breakfast and supper last night! Is everything okay?"

She hugs me, and I return it easily. She's a great hugger. If I had a favourite aunt or grandmother, I'd like to imagine they'd hug just like Millie.

"Yes, I'm fine. I had a long day and fell asleep. I didn't hear a thing until this morning."

She doesn't believe me. Her eyes say so like a beacon on a lighthouse.

Liar, liar.

"Will you come for supper tonight? It's homemade stew and bread. If you're around this afternoon, I'll even show you how to make the bread. Another cooking lesson if you'd like."

God dammit. Even Millie has that hopeful look in her eye.

"I need to visit the town and check my emails, but I'll be here for supper, for sure. I'll try to get in a bread lesson if Pete gets me back in time."

Millie pats my cheek and hands Pete her list and we're back outside again. No bus today, instead it's Pete's own pickup truck. Once we're inside and on the road, I interrogate Pete.

"You knew Millie would make me feel guilty for not being there last night, didn't you?"

"Sure did." He darts a glance at me. "She's attached to you. You have a way about you, Sasha, that everyone loves. You get into their hearts just by being yourself. I don't think you know that."

"Just get right to it, why don't you?" I grumble.

He chuckles. "You started it. But I had to step in. You look like you're about to do something stupid." More serious this time, he spares a quick glance my way. "Are you, Sasha?"

"Depends what you think stupid is, I guess."

He nods and the truck bumps along the road. My stomach tightens the longer I'm in this space with Pete, with nothing to distract me from Leaf.

"You owe him nothing, Sasha. None of us, really. You've been here, what? Three and a half weeks? You could be just another guest at the lodge, but you're not. However, if that's what you want to remain, we shouldn't pressure you into anything more."

First Perry, then Millie, now Pete. I can ignore all their comments and actions that show they care, but I can't ignore Leaf's.

"I owe him everything. That's where you're wrong, Pete." Staring out the window, I watch the trees pass by and not for the first time, I wonder if I really could fit in here.

When Pete pulls in front of the coffee shop, I blink. I must have zoned out the rest of the drive here.

"I figured this is where you'd like to start. You missed coffee this morning."

Pete still smiles, and with a wink he gets out, so I do the same.

"What time do you want to meet back here?"

The coffee shop door jingles as we enter and the heavenly smell of chocolate and coffee slams into me.

"How about 2 P.M.? Is that enough time for you to do what you need?"

Now that I know I don't need time to rebook a flight and get the hell out of here, I nod. "I should be done by then. Thanks."

Pete is all smiles as he gets the brownie he loves and leaves with a wave. I settle at a table looking out to the bookshop across the street with a mocha latte that's heaven in a cup and a slice of sugar pie. After setting up my laptop and connecting to the Wi-Fi, I hesitate.

I should call Roman first. When he doesn't pick up, I finally click the email icon and watch all the messages load. There's so many. Some with those annoying little red exclamation marks to signal it's more important than the others. Savouring the forkful of pie, I wonder who thought those little red marks were a good idea.

Ignoring all of them for now, I sign into my student account at the college. I'm enrolled in a photography program that I'm due to begin in September. Being in front of the camera is what I'm known for, but being behind it is a passion that's grown over the years. After reviewing all the course requirements and deadlines, I'm no closer to deciding what I'll do when I leave Maple Mountain Lodge.

Well, I have a plan, but now it's complicated, with an incredibly kind and handsome lumberjack who probably doesn't need my kind of mess in his life.

Flipping back to my email, I scroll until I find the ones from my lawyer. It's been great not being tied to the laptop and all the bullshit I'm still dealing with concerning Moe. My hand shakes as I lift the coffee cup and I wish Roman would pick up the phone.

As if he knows I need him, my phone rings and in my haste, I slosh coffee on the table reaching for it.

"Ro?"

"Sorry. I was in the middle of a shoot. Are you okay?"

"Okay." I huff a breath while trying to hang on to the thread of sanity I have left. "I'm still here and wondering how much longer this will drag out. I... I want to get on with my life, but I don't want to drag anyone into this shit."

"Oh, Sash. What happened?"

"The damn lumberjack, is what happened. I think he has feelings for me."

Roman snorts and I scowl.

"Darn. I hate it when attractive men want to have more with me. It's such a hardship."

"Don't be an asshole, Ro. I can't do this, can I?"

"Do what exactly?"

"Have a normal life. Maybe fall in love. Get a dog or some shit like that."

Never have I allowed myself to dream that I could have it all. The family and white picket fence. Maybe 2.5 kids and soccer practice. I've never had that kind of normality. Leaf is like an oasis come to life. All of that could be mine if I could just shake the notion that I don't deserve it.

"You can do it all, Sasha. Don't let that asshole take it all away from you. It's almost over. My lawyer said it will be over quicker if we both show up, give our statements, and no more lawsuits. He's done."

"I'll be back in a few days. The last email didn't give a date."

"He said to let him know once you're back and he'll set it up."

My hand slides into my hair, and I tug at the strands. "It's a guarantee, right? This is the end of it?"

"Yeah. And then you're gonna ride off into the sunset with your lumberjack. Does he have a brother?"

"He does, but you won't like him."

"Solomon Montpellier! Bite your tongue! You know I like them big and strong."

My lips twitch in a small smile.

"You're incorrigible. And I need you to be serious."

"For you I will be. Fire away."

"If Leaf has feelings and I don't have this all wrong... how do I, like... I don't know how to love someone back, Ro. I'm terrified of hurting him. He already lost a husband. What if I get it all wrong?"

"There's literally no right or wrong way, Sasha. And if you're asking how to do it, my guess is you're wondering how you can make it work already. It's scary. I've never been in love either, except that one time I found that gorgeous red Italian silk. That was real love. But if he's making you feel things new and scary, I think you owe it to yourself to try."

"Isn't there a textbook I could read or something?"

He laughs with a small sigh. I'm kidding, but only partly. Isn't there a book on this kind of thing?

"Maybe, but go with your gut."

"My gut got me into this mess."

"That's different. Being manipulated by Moe is something you never could have predicted. I need you to promise me something, Sasha."

"Anything."

"Talk to Leaf. Please don't just run. It sounds like he's a wonderful man and if he loves *this* Sasha? This new version of you who you also love? Don't let it pass, my friend. Life is hard enough on your own. If you found someone to be with, jump in."

"Damn you for making sense."

He laughs, "Now about this brother..."

"I'll fill you in when I'm home, Ro. I've got some thinking to do and I'll call you when I land."

"Call me anytime. I love you."

"Thanks. I love you too."

Draining my cup, I check the time. First the bookstore, then the pharmacy.

Then it's time to think.

Chapter 16
Leaf

Replacing the bandage on my thumb, I pause and stare at the man in the mirror. The sleep deprived and shadowed eyes of a man who laid awake most of the night stare back. It's been a long time since I've looked this rough.

After knocking on Sasha's door for more time than I want to admit, and being ignored, I spent the night in my hammock with the stars. Lost in thoughts about my past and future, I hoped to wish on a shooting star that I wasn't about to walk the path of grief once again. Not even a wink of sleep happened.

How could I sleep when I'd allowed my heart and thoughts to twist into a complicated knot that gripped my entire being?

And now I'm in an awkward place. Finally stepping away from the loss of Connor, and what I hoped was into something to bring light to my days and joy to my heart. But after Sasha not answering me—and I know he heard me knocking—I have to face the reality that maybe I jumped in too fast. He has a lot to look forward to and why would he want to put himself at my lodge when he's used to the glamour of the city?

"You look like shit." I mutter, running a hand down my face.

The chime of my doorbell has my heart leap to my throat and I rush to answer it.

"Oh. Hey."

Not who I was hoping for, as Perry brushes by me.

"Gee, thanks for the warm welcome, brother." He heads to my fridge as I close the door with a sigh.

"Sorry. Thanks for coming over."

He pauses before drinking from the can of ginger ale. "You look like shit. Talk to me."

"Thanks for noticing."

Leaning against the counter, he waits while I try to form a sentence that sums up what's eating away at me.

"He didn't let me in last night. I haven't slept."

Perry cocks his head. "Did he know you were there?"

"He knew I'd be coming. Maybe he fell asleep." I trail off, looking away from my brother's pity face.

"Leaf..." he sighs and raises his hands in a gesture to calm me down. It backfires. I know that tone and I won't forgive him if he's the reason for me laying awake all night.

"What did you do, Perry? What now? Why can't you just stay out of my life for once?!"

My voice booms in the small space and Perry slams his hand on the island in an uncharacteristic show of anger. He's always the calm one, and any more accusing words towards him die on my lips.

"You're not the only one who lost someone when Connor died, Leaf."

Perry's voice is hard. Pained.

"I know you two got along like brothers. I'm sorry you miss him, too."

Perry steps towards me. Eyes glistening with unshed tears.

"No, Leaf. You still don't get it." He swallows hard. "When he died, you went with him. I lost my brother." His voice hitches. "For seven fucking years, I've tried and hoped you'd come back. But you never did. You just folded farther and farther into yourself and I couldn't do a damn thing about it."

His voice drops, and for the first time since Connor died, I notice the real Perry. The pain in his voice is just like mine, and I regret yelling earlier.

"My brother was still here in body, but *you* weren't really here. We stopped meeting for beers. You didn't even talk shit about the *Habs* losing all the time whenever I was in the room." I'm alarmed at the tears on his cheeks. "You shut me out, Leaf. And I want my brother back. Sasha brought my brother back. I told him that."

"Perry, I..."

"He doesn't think he belongs here, Leaf. I think he cares about you but is stuck on feeling... I don't know, left out."

"He said that?"

Perry shrugs and lets the fight drain from his body.

"Yeah and he gave me the impression he was about to bolt without a word, so I, well... I got mad."

With a heavy sigh, I run my hand through my hair.

"I don't know what to do. He has a life where he came from and I have one here. We knew that when we started this. I can't exactly stop him, can I? If he bolts, well, then I'll try to move on." Stepping closer to Perry, I pull him into a hug. "And I'll be the brother you miss again. Even if this doesn't work out, I know I've been distant. I'm sorry."

Perry hugs me tight and I silently berate myself for not noticing his burden sooner.

When we release each other, we're both a little wet around the eyes and we smile softly. If nothing else, this is good for our relationship, at least.

"Leaf, I don't know what's going on with him, but he's scared. Don't just let him walk away."

With a frustrated huff, I walk to the window.

"He has a life. I can't handcuff him and keep him."

Believe me, I thought about it last night.

"Do you know why he'd be so scared and want to run without a word to you? I'm pretty oblivious to most things, but you two really connected. If I wanted to be all fucking sentimental about it, I'd say something more profound, but I'm not big on the mushy stuff." He shrugs with a smile.

"His mother died when he was still a child. He was only thirteen and with no other family, a friend of his mother's offered to take him in instead of going to foster care."

Foster care would likely have been a better choice. If I ever cross paths with this Moe person, well, let's just say I know how to make things look like an accident.

"The so-called friend used him. He recognized Sasha had a quality he could sell. Which was how he started modelling. But he... there was a lot more to it, Perry. I don't want to disclose it all, but I think it's hard for him to believe in love when he's only ever had it from his mother. Every single person in his life has lied and used him. I think maybe he can't trust so easily."

Perry curses under his breath.

"Jesus. I'm sorry, bro. Fuck..." His hands clench into fists and I know Perry feels the same as me. He can hear the words I'm not saying.

Moe kept Sasha on a leash until he was seventeen. That's when Sasha put the pieces together and found out what Moe was doing wasn't at all how business was supposed to work. Forced into bedrooms with grown men who should know better and led to believe it was the only way he could become successful. The extra incentives offered by Sasha Montpellier's agent landed him many deals, and not the talent he had. Or his natural beauty.

Fear had kept him silent.

When he could, he broke free at eighteen, only to sign with another sleazy agent who used him for himself. Sasha thought he cared about him as a person. That he truly loved him. The physical affection from the new agent was just another lie. It's no wonder he has a hard time trusting people. Meanwhile,

Sasha was once again tied to a contract with Moe through a third party. And then, when he broke his arm, all his problems with Moe came to a head.

"So, yeah. It has something to do with his past. It's been ten years since the worst of it, but I'm sure those scars don't fade easily."

"No, I imagine they wouldn't."

"And that's why I can't step in and beg him to stay, Perry. I don't want him to think I'm just like the rest."

"But you're not. You love him." He pauses. "Don't you?"

"I don't know if I'd call it love just yet, but I care. Far more than I should, probably. I could definitely see myself loving him if he'd let me."

"What can I do?"

Perry's tone pleads for something, but there's nothing he can do.

"Nothing Perry. You said your piece, and now it's up to him. I hope he'll talk to me before he leaves, at least."

I force a smile, but my eyes well at the thought of him leaving without a word.

Clearing my throat, I motion to the door. "I should probably get some work done. Checkouts and new arrivals need to be taken care of and I should make sure all my cleaning crew are on the board still."

Perry nods, striding to the door along with me, and he squeezes my shoulder.

"It will work out. It always does."

If it did, I wouldn't be a widower. But I'll keep that to myself for now and just hope this time things are different.

Hours have passed and I'm still in the office at the registration desk. I should really look at getting this stuff computerized. Piles of ledgers and receipts sit stacked all over the desk with rocks holding each pile down. An oversized box of paperclips and a heavy duty stapler sit nearby.

It's mind-numbing, but work that needs to be done. I'd much rather be on the lake or, hell, mowing the lawn. But not everything in business is glamorous.

"You know if you had a computer your life would have less paper cuts."

Startled by his voice, I whack my head off the side of the filing cabinet when I sit up.

"Ow, dammit."

Sasha's hand on my arm stops more expletives as I rub at my head. "Are you okay? I didn't mean to startle you."

"I'm okay. Not the first time I've done it."

The main door bangs behind him and Pete carries in a box to the kitchen. He nods with a sad smile towards Sasha.

"I'll be here for dinner tonight. Millie said she..." He trails off with a shake of his head. "I miss you. I'm sorry I didn't answer last night." His voice fades away as he steps back.

"I understand."

Please step closer.

"I don't think you do. And I... can we talk tonight?"

Will you tell me you'll stay?

"Of course."

My replies are very robotic, but he seems unsettled. Like a rabbit in the woods about to careen off into the bushes before he gets his wits about him.

His flirty smile returns, and I notice how he appears less like a city dweller today. With a quick perusal, I take in the new running shoes, nothing fancy, but he definitely bought them here. They go well with his cutoff jean shorts that show more skin than denim and his t-shirt is a plain white tee. But the ball cap he sets on his head is also new and my heart soars with the hope that this is his first attempt to blend in with the locals.

"Good. I look forward to it." He leans in and presses up on his toes to kiss my cheek. "See you later, Leaf."

He hikes his backpack up on his shoulder and leaves me standing there, staring after one of the many layers of Sasha.

Slumping back in the desk chair, I return to my organizing and paper piling. Stapling and stacking in the boxes next to me. After my third paper cut and another bandage, I yank open the desk drawer and shove around the contents until I find the business card I hoped was still there.

Dialing the number from the cordless phone in the office, I pace while waiting for the call to be picked up.

"Evergreen Communications, how can I help you?"

"Uh, hi. This is Leaf Attwater at Maple Mountain Lodge. You dropped by a few years ago to talk about internet and cell service and… well, I never called you back. Is it still an option?"

"If I remember, you pushed me out the front door and said your system was fine as is. But of course it's still an option. In fact, there's a better option now. When can I come by to do an assessment?"

"As soon as you can would be preferable."

"That's a mighty big change in attitude, but I'll be there Friday afternoon if that works?"

"It will work just fine. Thank you."

After confirming numbers and information, I stand there staring out the tiny office window for a long time. Friday works. It will give me something to focus on when Sasha walks out of my life.

All I can hope is that it won't be forever.

Chapter 17
Sasha

My time here is almost up, and it's passed in a blur. Or does it just seem that way because I'm not ready to go back?

Back to the reality of a boring new life as a student and, hopefully, an entrepreneur. But not until I deal with the nastiness of Moe and finally putting that to rest. Every time I have to see him in court, it sends me into such a tailspin. My fear is that I might take longer to bounce back this time.

Until that question is answered, I won't lay it at Leaf's feet. I just hope he understands why.

And Roman was wrong.

I found a book today about how to love. Well, kind of. Self-help books are just as plentiful as the swoony romances I lose myself in. While they give me an escape and a hope that one day I'll find my prince charming, they don't really help me work toward the problem I keep avoiding.

My long-time therapist always tells me I have to work on believing I'm worthy and to continue being myself no matter what. But ever since Moe brainwashed me into believing I was only good for sex and posing in front of a camera, my sense of self disappeared. Buried so deep, even a cadaver dog can't find it.

I spent years drifting from man to man with the belief I wasn't good enough. I wasn't smart enough or worthy of anything that even resembled love. The only love I knew and trusted was my mother's, and she wasn't here to help. Nor could a mother's love compare to the love of a romantic partner.

But it was something. A small thread to remember what it felt like to be loved just as I was. That thread was getting shorter as more time passed. I was slipping away.

I came here to find the part of me that was missing. The confidence that I was capable and deserving of anything good. And to be fair, I owed it to myself to try all the things I'd been told I couldn't do. Without the fear of repercussions. There were no contracts to lose or people to disappoint. It's just me, and I need this.

Stepping onto the porch, I settle on the swing and crack the spine of a book I hope might help. Therapy has been great, but it's not like I can walk around with my therapist to reassure me I'm a good person and deserve good things. The answer is likely not in this book either, but it's a start.

A pair of chipmunks chirp and chase each other in front of the tiny porch. They chase each other in circles around a tree before diving into the bushes nearby. A moment later, one emerges with a peanut lodged in its cheeks and, unbidden,

I laugh out loud. The chipmunk startles and, with its full cheeks, it scampers off into the brush again.

"I like that sound."

Leaf stands at the edge of the path leading to my cabin, hands in his pockets and looking oh so damn perfect with his rolled-up sleeves and faded jeans. It's the middle of July. How he always wears jeans, I can't understand. Must be something lumberjack-ish.

"The chipmunks? Yeah, they're cute."

"No, your laugh." He steps closer until he stands at the bottom of the porch steps. "And your face when you let it out when you thought no one was watching."

Oof. That's a direct hit to my feels.

"What exactly did you like? I sound like a hyena on helium."

Leaf shakes his head with a soft smile.

"I liked that it was all you. For ten seconds, you were one hundred percent lost in what was around you and your eyes lit up while your lips kinda twitched." He steps up on the porch and hesitates before sitting on the other half of the porch swing with me. "You were, for one stolen moment, the real Sasha. Open and without worry or burden. And..." he dips his head with a small puff of air. "You're beautiful."

He casts a sideways glance and my heart melts.

"I just wanted to come by to see you." He brushes his hand on my thigh. "Take a break from all the paper cuts."

Biting my lip, I look away from his handsome face. His candidness is hard for me to manage right now. His words drip with sincerity and a longing I crave, but no idea how to accept.

"You have a lovely town here." Deflection is my best defence. "I met some great people at the bookstore."

"They're amazing people. It's a nice town. Winters are long, but it's a slice of paradise here."

Again, a smile twitches on my lips. He seems to make that happen to me more.

"Indeed. There's the best maple syrup I've ever tasted here."

Leaf huffs a small laugh and allows the silence to bind us together. I know he wants to say more, as do I, but I don't have the confidence to ask the questions. And I don't know how to handle the words he might say.

Leaf must sense my turmoil. He stands, lightly squeezing my leg before he does.

"I won't keep you from your book. I just wanted to see you." With a sigh, he walks the steps to the trail back to the lodge. Before he disappears, I call out.

"Leaf! I'll be there for dinner."

His shoulders relax, and a happy smile fills his face.

"I'll see you then."

And he leaves me on the porch staring at the blurry pages of a book I hoped to find the answers in. But even I know a book won't help.

Dinner is loud with all the chatter of the lodge guests. Groups of men and women talk about the fish they caught today. Somebody named Jack caught a record-setting pike! I don't know what that means, but it's hard not to feel the excitement in the air.

I slide into a corner by myself at the end of a bench with a large group. They may as well be speaking a different language with all the fishing terms and slang they're throwing around. I smile and laugh when they do, and they include me in their conversations.

The entire time, my gaze keeps landing on Leaf as he floats around the tables, mingling with the groups that are due to checkout tomorrow along with me. He's very popular. People flag him down at every step and there's a few I notice he touches more. Friendly, like he genuinely cares about them, and I wonder if those are people who return every year.

"Do you leave tomorrow, too?"

It's the man next to me, and I notice the group I'm sitting with is starting to disperse.

"I do."

"Me too. Our group does. We've been coming here every year since it opened. Leaf is amazing. Have you met him?"

I almost laugh out loud at his question, but keep it in.

"I have. He's a great guy."

"One of the best men I've ever met. I'm pleased he kept the place open after his husband died. I think it's good for him to see everyone, you know? We're not his family, but coming back here always feels like visiting family."

"Monty! I didn't get to spend much time with you this week." Leaf seats himself across from the man. "I've been busy meeting new people." He winks at me and my cheeks flame.

Monty laughs a hearty laugh. "I should hope so, Leaf. We love coming to see you, but we know how it works. How have you been? You seem happier." He reaches over and squeezes Leaf's hand. "It looks good on you, son."

Leaf doesn't hide his fondness for Monty. He squeezes his hand back with a smile.

"I am happier, Monty. Time to get back to living. That's what Connor would want. Just took me a longer time to accept it, I guess."

"I know what you mean. When I lost my Lucy, I never thought the sun would shine again. It was a dark time. But I finally started seeing someone. Her name is Darla, and she's one of the prettiest ladies I've ever met. Cooks a mean lemon pie, too."

Monty smiles tenderly at Leaf. It's obvious they're close. Monty's eyes shine with unshed tears and I quietly excuse myself from their moment.

Dropping my plate in the collection bin, I spy Millie and give her a wave. She immediately pulls me into the kitchen with her.

"I missed you this afternoon. I thought you wanted to make bread?"

"Ah, crap. It slipped my mind. I'm sorry, Millie."

"Oh, not to worry. An old lady sometimes gets her hopes up is all. I saw you talking with Monty. He's a sweet man. His wife used to come with him and she'd just sit near the docks with knitting on the sunny days. If it was raining, she'd sometimes ask to help in the kitchen since she loved to cook and she didn't want to watch TV all day."

"What happened to her?"

Millie squeezes my hand and the sadness in her voice breaks my heart.

"Cancer. It was quick at least, but we sure were shocked when Monty called to tell us. I'm happy he started coming back with his old crew, though."

"He and Leaf are close, aren't they?"

She nods, the sadness clearing from her voice.

"Oh yes. He was here a few weeks after Connor died. He was just as crushed about it as the rest of us. Monty insisted on getting Leaf out of his suite and took him on the boat. It was the first time Leaf had even left the building after the funeral. So, yeah, Monty is a special, special man."

She motions for me to come closer to the giant fridge.

"I made something for you to take home tomorrow." She presents me with a small box.

"Oh, thank you. You didn't have to do that."

"I know, but I wanted to."

Flipping open the lid, my mouth waters when I smell maple syrup.

"You made me maple cookies? Oh my god! This is amazing! Thank you!"

Launching myself at her, I hug her hard and feel the lump building in my throat.

"Of course I did."

A throat clears behind us and Leaf leans against the doorway with a small smile.

"Ah, she made you maple crème cookies. You must be high in Millie's books. She doesn't make those for just anyone. Including me."

"Oh shush. You can have them whenever you want, Leaf."

"I'll hold you to it, Millie." He nods to the doorway hidden off in the corner. "Do you still want to come up?"

"Of course." I hug Millie once more and she whispers in my ear.

"I hope we see you back, love. Keep in touch."

"I will. Bye, Millie."

Leaf holds the door open for me and, clutching the box of cookies to my chest like a sugary shield, I climb the dark staircase to the top where the other door to Leaf's place awaits.

Once inside, I'm immediately swamped with sadness. Its fingers curl into me with a tight grip I find hard to shake off.

"Sasha, please. Let's talk."

Still holding my cookies, I perch on Leaf's sunrise loveseat. The sun still shines, not quite ready to disappear behind the treetops and, for now, the room still has a natural light.

Leaf sits next to me and gently takes the cookie box, setting it on the table.

"Can I go first? I have so much I want to say to you, and it feels like I don't have enough time."

"Funny, I was just thinking that today, too."

Leaf's eyes soften, and he takes my hand in his.

"You're the first person who I've felt like giving myself to since Connor died. It's not an easy spot to be in. I know you might think you can't replace him and you're right. Nobody ever will. But what I've only come to realize myself is that I can still love him and love someone else, too." He reaches over, brushing a thumb over my cheek. "I have room in my heart for that. I'd like to let you have it."

"Why me?" I take his hand in mine, pressing it against my chest. "I know I asked you not to hurt me, but Leaf... what if I hurt you because this is all new to me? How can you want me when all I've been to others is a throwaway toy? I'm not special."

His brow knits and a storm swirls in his eyes.

"You've been with the wrong people. I know there's lots you've held back from me. And I hope you'll tell me when you're ready, but you *are* special. Don't you see? You made me laugh just by being you and yes, you're a very attractive man. You woke me up again, Sasha. I want to be with you, kiss you, get to know you. I wish I'd been able to take you out on the lake again. You did that. I don't think you realize how special that makes you."

He means it too. His words wrap around me and try to stick. I want them to, but it's hard.

"I have to go home to take care of... not nice things. Embarrassing things. I'd like to tell you about them one day, with all the details. But I'm ashamed of it, that's the truth, and I'm used to doing things alone."

"C'mere."

Leaf holds his arm up and lowers himself onto the loveseat, inviting me to snuggle under his arm. With a sad smile, I lay my head on his chest while his hand smoothes my back. The steady beat of his heart against my cheek is a reminder that this man is real. Screw the shame and embarrassment. He's here for me. If there's anytime to be brave, it's now. And before I can stop myself, I'm spilling my guts about the abuse someone else presented proof of and the sentencing hearing waiting for me when I get home.

Through hitched breaths and tears, I tell Leaf everything I've ever left out. From how Moe stole most of my earnings by lying to me outright and dipped into the small trust fund that was left behind from a life insurance policy my mother had with me as the beneficiary. How he first convinced me to have sex with casting agents as a normal part of the business. Finally, once I figured out it wasn't normal practice, how he then coerced me with threats of having no money to sustain myself. I did the lowest thing imaginable and let him into my bed for fear of being homeless and alone. I let him use me so I could keep a roof over my head and have a job.

Only Roman and the lawyer know that part. I've never shared that with anyone else.

"Sasha... are you sure you want to face this man alone? You don't have to."

"Roman will be with me. He stole from Roman's accounts—and a few others— too. I was the lucky one who had to see him naked, though."

A growl from Leaf has my shoulders tense. His arm tightens around me.

"Please let me come to you, Sasha." His voice shakes and I push up to look into his face. He wipes the tears from my cheeks while his eyes beg for me to let him help. "Your friends, I'm sure, are amazing, but I don't want you to be alone."

"It's not your mess, though. It's mine to clean up."

"Sasha..."

"I promise I'll try to come back. You're the only one I've ever shared all this with. I'm still working out things, but... I don't want you to be there while I do. I hope you can understand."

He sits up, pressing his lips to mine in a kiss that almost makes me change my mind and beg him to come with me.

"I do, baby. Doesn't mean I like it."

"Can I... would it be okay for me to spend the night here?"

Leaf studies me in that way that makes me feel naked. Completely exposed inside and out.

"Is that all you want?"

His hand cups my cheek, and I lean into his touch.

"I wouldn't mind it if you showed me again how special I am. I mean... only if you want to. I know you're not like the others, Leaf. I feel it every time you touch me. I'd like to leave here with that feeling."

He stares at me for so long I think he'll change his mind. Perhaps it's all too much for him now that it's out there and he thinks I'm not worth the effort. But he doesn't change his mind.

Instead, he stands, pulling me up to him.

"I want you to leave here and never forget me. Because no matter what happens, I won't forget you."

Chapter 18
Leaf

This has the potential to kill me. But I can't let Sasha leave here without setting his mind at ease that he's so much more than a pretty face and a willing body.

He's pure and smart and he spreads light everywhere he goes.

And I've likely fallen in love with him.

I wasn't expecting that. Not with the memories of Connor still so close. Seven years hasn't lessened my love for him, but it's tiring being alone, pining for someone who died. I filled my recent sleepless night with more than wishing on stars. For the first time since I lost the love of my life, I forced myself to face the stirrings in my soul. To listen to my heart when it said I may be lucky enough to find another love.

Sasha hasn't been here long, but I don't need more time to know how I feel. Just like there's no time limit on grief, there's none for love. It's a shock when you realize that elusive emotion, that soul binding love you should only have once, has appeared again when you weren't even looking.

But he's not ready.

If he wants me to make him never forget this connection we've forged, then I will. Because I want the same thing, even if it means I'll never see him again.

Once in my bedroom, he waits as I light a candle. I read it was romantic to have candles during sex. Since he likes romance, I planned ahead, hoping we'd end up here. But not in this manner. Something a little less sad because he can't wait to come back would be my preference. But if a promise of him trying and a request to make him remember is all I get, then it's time to pull out all the stops.

Sasha doesn't let me get much farther than lighting a candle before he's pulling at my clothes, unbuttoning my shirt and laying soft kisses on my chest.

"Why do you always wear long sleeves? It's July."

Grinning as I pull off his shirt, I answer with a small laugh.

"It's sun protection. It's light. I'm never hot."

"You're always hot."

He raises a saucy eyebrow, and I laugh again. God, he makes me laugh so easily.

"I'm glad you think so."

Sasha smiles, the earlier melancholy gone, and takes my face in his hands. His lips whisper across mine before he kisses me. Deep and so tender, I'm left breathless.

"I think so much of you, Leaf." He rests his forehead on my shoulder, placing a kiss there. "I'm afraid to admit you're maybe the perfect man for me."

My fingers flex on his hips.

"Nobody's perfect," I kiss his temple, "but we could be damn close to it together."

His lips take mine again and we say nothing more. He doesn't have to, because I feel it in every touch and every kiss. And it breaks my heart that he thinks he doesn't deserve to have this with me. That he can't trust me all the way to help him through his dark times.

Hot and naked, both of us tumble onto the bed. Sasha slithers down my body, kissing me on every exposed inch of my body, leaving a trail of gooseflesh in his wake. Every cell of my body sings for him and cries out to stay connected for as long as possible.

His tongue licks and swirls around my cock and I push up on my elbows to watch. He puts on a show for me, never breaking eye contact as he sucks me down. Those eyes... fuck, they say so much and again I wish desperately for him to see in himself what I see.

"Come up, here. I want to taste you, too."

Sasha slides up my body, his hard cock pressing against mine. Something changed. He feathers a kiss on the corner of my mouth.

"Can I do this?" He whispers. "Be on top?"

"Of course you can. I'd never say no to that."

His hands shake as he caresses my chest and I stare into his beautiful eyes. He opens his mouth and closes it. No words come, so I offer my own.

"Don't explain, babe." My palm slides across his cheek, thumb grazing his puffy lower lip. "I'll never deny you."

He swallows hard and I wish I could wash away all the doubts. I've never had to wrestle with his kind of demons, though. A love lost through death differs from never believing you're worthy of it.

The ache to tell him to stay is so fierce, I reach up and pull his mouth to mine.

"Do what you want, Sasha. I'm yours."

Gasping, he tears his mouth from mine. Cheeks flushed and eyes ablaze, he slides back down my body and kneels between my legs. He doesn't touch me. Sasha's chest heaves as he stares at my painfully hard cock and I'm not sure where his mind went, but I bend my knees and open my legs farther. I'm not sure how much more of an invitation he'd like, but I don't have time to engrave one.

"Sasha..." He snaps his eyes to mine. "I don't want to rush you, but I'm getting a little impatient. Can you please do something? Suck my dick, touch my balls, literally anything, because I'm burning up with you sitting there just out of reach and staring."

"Sorry." He whispers.

"Don't be sorry. Just... do something." I huff a tense laugh because I want this to be what he wants. His control. His choice. But I'm also a man who wants to come sometime this evening.

Sasha listens to my plea, and he shocks me by spreading my cheeks and rimming me to an inch of my life.

"Holy shit... Sasha ...*fuuuck*."

When he finally comes up for air, the triumphant smile on his face leaves me breathless. Saliva-soaked, reddened lips grin at me with a debauched tilt.

"I've always wanted to do that."

"Well, shit. If I knew that, I'd have volunteered earlier."

He laughs, deep and throaty, and I know now that I'd do anything to hear it again.

"I'll mark it down that you approve. Hopefully, I can add the next thing to your list of volunteer activities."

He coats my cock in lube and positions himself, sinking down slowly until he's panting, fully impaled on me. After adjusting a few times, he rocks his hips with a moan and plants his hands on my chest.

"Leaf... holy crap..."

He throws his head back, lost in the act of flesh on flesh and chasing his orgasm. I close my hand on his dick and he gasps.

"Is this okay?"

"Yes." It's but a hiss and he sits up farther, giving me room to jerk him while he rides me. "I'm gonna come. Holy..."

He doesn't finish the sentence because he tenses and with a gasp, he coats me with his cum. It's in my beard and on my chest, and Sasha grins like a fool. A beautiful, blissed out fool.

"You look amazing in everything you wear, but this?" He gestures to the mess he made on me. "This is my favourite."

"You like me covered in your spunk, do you?"

"Sure do." He rocks back on my dick and I groan. "And I want you to fill me with yours."

He collapses forward, kissing me, not caring he now has cum on his face and I lift my hips, chasing my orgasm that hovers so close.

"You sure?" I pant into his mouth.

"Very. I want a part of you. Please, Leaf."

With a shudder and groan, my orgasm slams into me and Sasha shakes as I grip his hips, holding him there. He kisses my neck, my cheek and lips, and spears his fingers in my hair.

We take a moment to catch our breath and the reality that he'll be gone in the morning is like a dagger in my heart and against my better judgement I say those words no one wants to hear after sex.

"I love you, Sasha."

His body tenses and I stroke his back as he buries his face in my neck. I don't expect him to say it back. I shouldn't have said it myself, but I know what it's like to wish you'd had one last chance to say the words in your heart.

In case he doesn't come back, I want him to know that at least once in his life someone who meant it loved him.

He kisses me, so soft it's like a breeze from a butterfly, before easing off my cock and lying next to me.

"Care to join me in the shower?"

Sasha floats a finger across my eyebrow and down my nose.

"I'd love to."

Setting out my fluffiest towels, I make sure the water runs warm before we step inside. We steal kisses and touches as we take turns lathering each other up. Even after our emotionally charged sex, we still kiss and touch, exploring this connection we have. Sasha remains mostly quiet, but his silence is louder than any words he could say. He washes my beard with a reverence that takes my breath away. So much so that it's almost my undoing.

Instead of words, all I can do is hold him against me and feel his heart beat with mine. Once we're back under the covers, I know once I fall asleep, it's the last time I'll see him.

Call it a feeling, but this was our goodbye.

As expected, I wake up alone.

I should be angry I couldn't send him off, but I'm glad. Sort of. He did it his way. The silliest thing about it all is I'm just happy I could give him what he came here for. Perhaps even more.

The ache of him leaving will linger, but I've been through worse. It's because of him I know I can. Weird, but when does life ever make any sense?

He left me a note with his phone number and drew a big heart around it. Which I'm probably reading more into than I should.

A knock on my door pulls me from my thoughts and I set the note aside.

"Pete. Hi. Come in."

"I just wanted to drop by and check on you."

Nodding, I sigh. "Well, I'm here. And... how was he?"

He runs a hand over his face. "A shadow of himself, Leaf. What the hell happened?"

I motion for Pete to have a seat at the kitchen island and pour him a coffee before settling across from him.

"Everything and nothing, Pete. I may have got too close and scared him, or I got just close enough for him to spread his wings and fly."

Pete, the straight talking man I've always known him to be, nods and sets his mug aside.

"Excuse me, boss, but why aren't you flying with him?"

"What do you mean?"

"I've watched him the few times I took him to town. How eager he was to visit the shops on the main street. He fell in love with the coffeehouse. And if I'm not wrong, he maybe fell in love with this place, too." He sips his coffee again, peering over the top of his mug. "Or someone maybe?"

Pete doesn't miss much. He and Millie and my brother know me the best, but Pete talks to me no-nonsense. Straight up. Not like Perry, who's always swinging, wanting to take down anything that might cause me pain. Pete has a gentle touch, and he gets the more emotional side of me.

"Maybe. A guy can hope, right? It's not wrong of me to hope."

He taps his fingers on the counter before pulling out a small package from his pocket. "He asked me to give this to you."

He hands me a small package, the size of a paperback. It's wrapped in a brown shopping bag and scrawled on the front of it, simply *For Leaf.*

"He didn't tell me what it was, but he was very insistent that I deliver it as soon as I got back."

Turning it over in my hands, I'm filled with a longing to have the time roll back. To have Sasha on the boat or see him laughing at chipmunks. To feel the weight of him next to me while we lay in bed.

"Hey, you call me if you need me." Pete says in a soft voice. "I'll let you open that in private."

Startled at the wetness in my eyes, I nod.

"Thanks, Pete. I will."

He lets himself out and leaves me to my thoughts. Sitting on the loveseat, I take a breath before sliding the paper off the package. It's a photo album. One made to fit 4x6 photos, and a laugh bubbles out at the title he's scrawled across the front.

In my lumberjack era.

Flipping through the pages, he's made me a scrapbook of his time here. There are photos of our time on the boat, me chopping wood, and photos around the lodge. He's written little notes along the few lines at the side of each picture of his memories. Some are little poems, other are little doodles with hearts and smiley faces.

But it's the final photo that stops me in my tracks.

A selfie taken together along the beach one evening. The sun is just setting, and it's a gorgeous red-orange glow. Our cheeks were supposed to be pressed together, but a loon called and Sasha turned his head to look for it. It's there in the background as he looks out after it. But my expression in the photo is what I'm focused on.

Running my fingers across the photo, I almost don't recognize the joy, but it's right there.

His note says, *Find yourself a lumberjack who looks at you like this.*

And the hesitation I've felt since Connor died melts a little more.

There's something I need to do.

Before I can talk myself out of it or overthink it, I quickly change and rush out to my truck.

Chapter 19
Leaf

S itting on the same park bench I shared with Sasha a short time ago, I bounce the tiny photo album on my lap. People walk by like any other weekday. Joggers run through Connor's park, their conversations barely breathless as they run by.

And I tune it all out. I'm here with Connor.

While I avoided coming here for years since they dedicated it to him, I prefer it over visiting his headstone. This is Connor. The green space. The people and birds. All the things he loved and lived for. And if I expect him to talk to me, it will probably happen here.

"I think you know how much I miss you, Con." I whisper to the water in the small creek that runs through the park. He always wanted the town to have a skating pond on it, but the current was always strong enough that the ice was never safe for use. The creek often had open water through the winter, so it wasn't possible.

"I know you can't come back to me. I stopped wishing for that a long time ago. But I never want to forget you. And it took me seven long years, but I finally realized I can still have you and let someone else in."

Flipping open the album Sasha left, I turn to one of my favourites. It's on the boat and Sasha took my photo while I was laughing at something. It'd been years since I smiled and laughed so much, but his caption stuck with me.

The joy in your smile has a story, and I felt it.

And of course, that final photo with the damn loon in the background. I can't stop looking at it and wondering...

"Con, was that you? Do you know? I know you loved watching the loons and I remember that one night on the lake. Remember? You had that wildlife seminar and you went on and on with your loon facts." I stop to laugh and wipe away a tear. I can still hear his voice from that night.

"Leaf, did you know when a loon's eyes are red it's a sign they're still in mating season?"

"I'm pretty sure they're always red, baby."

"No, look at that one!"

He points to a loon off the bow of the boat and hands me the binoculars.

"Okay, so it doesn't have red eyes."

"That one found its mate."

"Is that what I am? Your mate?"

I nuzzle into his neck and he gently pushes me away.

"You are until something happens to one of us. Loons don't mate for life, but they're monogamous when they find a mate. Sometimes they get pushed out by other males or one of the pair

dies, but when they're together for the season, they look out for each other. They move on when things change."

"That's kind of sad, Con."

"I think it's perfect. If something happens to one of them, why should the other get left behind and live its life alone?"

"They're just birds."

"They're beautiful, smart birds and I think we can learn a little something from them. If something happened to you, I'd be like a loon. I'd hate to be without love again just because I lost one."

If only I knew then I'd not grow old with Connor maybe I'd have listened to his loon facts and not teased him. Yet now I'm here without Connor and finally getting what he was trying to tell me then.

"I might have found love again. Another loon." I chuckle to myself. "Well, he's not a loon, but you know what I mean. Because I think I finally get it, Con. You're right. Just like always. And I wanted to let you know because I always tell you everything. And it feels weird saying it out loud, but I think I'm in love. You'd like him. If you two met, I know you'd get into all kinds of trouble together."

A group of ducks swims out from under the bridge and I watch them swim by. As they swim around the bend, a single loon pops up from under the water. Time stands still as I gape at it and it bobs in the water, staring back at me.

Loons don't come here. They aren't good on land and need islands where it's harder for predators to get them. If you've ever seen a loon try to walk, you'd know why.

See, Con? I listened to some of your stuff!

"Con…"

I can't believe I'm talking to a fucking loon in a public park, but it doesn't move.

"Give me a sign if that's you, babe."

The loon bobs its head down once, twice, and my tears burst forth. This is impossible. My dead husband is not in the body of a loon.

But it's here. In *his* park where they never go.

"I love you. And I'm going to love him too. I wanted you to know."

The loon releases its well-known wail, much like a wolf howl that often signals to other loons where they are. The loon looks back towards the bridge when a loon call sounds in return. With a final moment staring at each other, it dives under the surface rather than swimming away.

I remain sitting on the bench for a long time, staring at the spot where the loon was and flipping through the photos Sasha left. It's only when the light rain starts that I return to my truck to drive home.

And once I'm there, I take the first step back to the Leaf I used to know.

The great thing about owning this lodge is I can find a million things to occupy my mind and not think of Sasha every minute. At least during the daytime.

At night, it's a different story.

It's only been three days since I woke up to find Sasha had snuck out, but it feels like three years.

Today's work also reminds me he's gone.

Painfully so.

The internet installer stands from the corner with a smile.

"Okay, we have the satellite on the roof and with the tower above the tree line, you should have a fairly reliable and stable connection for the internet and cell phones now." He offers his hand to shake. "Welcome to the 21st century." He laughs while I stare at all the equipment that now clutters my desk instead of paper. I may have gone a wee bit overboard in the technology department.

"It will save me from paper cuts, right? And hopefully free up time since I'm told a computer program is the way to go with bookkeeping these days."

The guy snorts and shakes his head.

"Now, with the satellite, you also get to have a cell phone tower signal. We have that set to bounce here for you, too." He takes out his cell phone and waits a second before a smile splits his face. "Ah-ha! You now get 3 bars of service. That's not too shabby for up here."

I'll take his word for it.

"Um, okay... could you help me figure this all out? You said I can connect the business through my phone? And get internet... on my phone?"

Snorting, he asks me to pass him the cell phone I bought two days ago along with the laptop, printer, router, and whatever the hell he had to install on my roof.

He talks the whole time about what he's doing and how it works, but it's honestly over my head. Worst case, I can get Perry over here to explain it when needed. He knows how to do all this techy shit.

When the man finally has me all set up and leaves, I stare at the laptop like it's a bomb ready to go off. He said I could take this upstairs and connect through Wi-Fi. Which means this list of passwords will need to come with me upstairs too.

Ignoring all the commotion for the approaching dinner service, I tuck the laptop, phone, and passwords under my arm and head up to my suite through the kitchen.

Millie gives me a nod and says nothing, which I'm grateful for. She likely knows what's driving my odd behaviour.

Once in my space, I heave a sigh of relief and collapse on the love seat.

Ever since the encounter with the loon at the park, I've been laser focused. To enjoy life and to move ahead. But it's tricky with Sasha.

He's so guarded. Far more than I ever was and with good reason. But it's been three days since I've heard his voice or seen his face. He left me his number for a reason. I wanted to video call, but Perry explained I would need to set up social media and a bunch of other stuff I wasn't keen on.

So I'm going the old-fashioned way and phoning him.

It rings four, five, six times before his voice mail picks up and when I hear his sweet voice, I sigh like a boy with a crush. The tone sounds and I stammer out a message.

"Um, hi. Sasha. It's me. Leaf. I'm leaving a message. Of course I am. Anyway, I... I miss you and I hope you call me back." I rattle off my number and say some other lame thing to end the call.

Feeling deflated that he didn't answer, I open the laptop, intent on figuring out all this social media stuff Perry told me about.

My phone rings before I get very far.

And it's Sasha.

Fumbling around, swiping to answer and silently cursing for a simpler phone, I hear his voice.

"Leaf! You got a cell phone?"

"Hello to you too, beautiful."

"Sorry, I just... I didn't think you had a cell. And... hi, I miss you too."

"I got it two days ago. And the guy was just here setting me up with, uh, a router and stuff. So the lodge has Wi-Fi and a decent cell signal now."

"Wow. That's very modern of you. What changed?"

I consider the best way to answer that and decide to go with the truth.

"I want to stay in touch with you. And also, I hate all the paper cuts I get when I do the books every month." Swallowing hard, I dare to say what I've been thinking about before he even left my bed. "But mostly because I hope it persuades you to come back."

I know he's there because I can hear him sniffle.

"Please tell me what it is, Sasha."

"Did you really mean what you said? Our last night, did you mean those words? Please be honest. I can handle it if it was just a heat of the moment thing."

"I have strong feelings for you, Sasha. That's very true. And I don't regret saying those words because you needed to know how I felt. I know you don't feel the same and that's okay."

My hands itch to just hold him next to me. His voice is good to hear, but I want so much more.

"I'm sorry I left you without saying goodbye. I knew I wouldn't be able to do it."

"I understand. I had a feeling you'd be gone when I woke up. I'm just glad you left me a number."

He yawns and apologizes, and there's a rustling noise.

"I don't want to keep you up. If you need sleep, I'll hang up... is it still called that on a cell phone?"

The sound of his laughter eases my sadness. And despite missing him, my lips find a way to smile.

"You still hang up, yes. End call is the term but the same thing. I can't wait for us to try texting." He laughs again and just hearing his joy makes my heart sing. Lord, I have it bad.

"How was your trip home?"

"They delayed the flight two hours out of Montreal. Then we had to wait for an hour to deplane when we landed because there weren't any bays for us to park at. Roman couldn't stay to wait for me since he had a commitment, but he arranged a car for me. I got home five hours later than I hoped and it just," I hear him swallow, fighting to keep it all in. "It was really trying, because this court thing is happening and my courses and my apartment... and then you. I'm really overwhelmed."

"What can I do to help you?"

He's silent for some time and I wait.

"Can you be patient?" His voice cracks. "Just... please wait for me to catch up, Leaf."

"If that's what you need and all I can do, then I will."

Jesus, the lump in my throat hurts.

"I should let you get your rest."

The silence hangs and foolishly; I don't want to be the one to say goodbye first. Hell, I don't ever want to say goodbye.

"Leaf?"

"Yeah?"

"Thank you. For everything. We'll talk again soon?"

"Call me anytime."

"I will."

"Until next time, then Sasha. Take care of yourself."

"I will. You too."

It's a fight, but I pull the phone from my ear and hit the end call button. I hear the beep in my ear signalling the call is over and lean back on the love seat.

My cell pings against my leg and when I glance down, it's my very first text message.

> **Beauty:** text me anytime. I answer texts before phone calls, lol. But I really am going to sleep now. xoxo

> **Leaf:** SLEEP WELL

> **Leaf:** I DON'T KNOW HOW TO TURN OFF THE CAP LOCK.

> **Beauty:** *laugh emoji*

And I still don't know how to get the text to not be in capitals, but it's another thing to add to my list for Sasha.

I don't care how long the list gets either.

Chapter 20
Sasha

"**S**asha! Open up! My hands are full and I don't want to set the food on the floor."

Roman's voice booms through my apartment door, and I bolt up from my bed. I slept for fourteen hours. How is that possible?

"Just a minute!"

Still in my boxers, I throw the blankets off and pad to the door. Roman stands in the hall with a tray of coffee and greasy breakfast food from the diner down the street.

"You look like shit, Sasha."

He brushes past me, his hair perfectly styled and eyeliner in place. Another impeccable outfit with dress pants that accentuate every desirable curve of my friend and his trademark business casual corset.

"Thanks, Ro. I'd love to say the same, but you look fucking incredible, as always."

He sets the food on the tiny table in my studio apartment and walks back to me.

"I'm not perfect and you know it. I also didn't spend a day on a plane travelling with a heavy heart. I'll look better than you without trying in that situation."

He laughs before hugging me and I hold on extra tight, relaxing into the familiar comfort of my best friend.

"I missed you, friend." He whispers against my cheek before releasing me.

"I missed you, too. And thank you for bringing food."

My belly rumbles in agreement, and we seat ourselves at the table. Roman unpacks my favourites from the diner. A toasted western sandwich on brown bread, tater tots, and bacon… extra soggy.

Four take out cups mean he brought me a plain old coffee and a mocha latté because he wasn't sure if I needed both. I'm not sure either, but I'll lean toward yes.

"So, what do you want to talk about first? The shit with Moe or the shit with your lumberjack?"

Roman grabs the apron hanging on the wall and puts it on before eating, and I raise an eyebrow.

He shrugs a shoulder. "I got a breakfast poutine. I don't want to spill. This is my favourite corset."

"Smart."

"I can be. So… talk to me."

Shovelling some of my favourite food into my mouth first, I watch as Roman carefully scoops a forkful of his messy breakfast into his mouth.

"Tell me about Moe first. When's the meeting?"

"Friday afternoon. We'll finish with his mess and go get wasted to celebrate. We'll be done with him, Sasha. This is the last time, and he won't get to hurt anyone else."

I release a huge breath. "Thank god. It would crush me to know he was still going around abusing kids like that. He should rot in hell."

I'm still pissed they said there wasn't enough evidence from me to press charges for abuse. At least I had enough evidence to get him for theft and removed from any position of authority with minors.

Roman shrugs and sips his coffee. "I'm sure hell is better than where he's going. Child abusers, even amongst criminals, have zero acceptance, you know. I'm happy he's finally off to where he belongs."

What? That's new information.

"I thought he was going to the white collar prison? It was only my word against his and I had no real proof."

Roman pauses and takes my hand.

"You didn't have proof, but someone else did."

The gravity of what he shares doesn't sit well. I know all of Moe's clients.

"Which one?" I whisper.

Roman sighs a shaky breath. "Lars. He met me at a shoot just after you left. He heard about the theft charges and asked me if there were other allegations or victims. He had a text exchange saved on his phone with Moe." Roman squeezes my hand again and looks away. He's sensitive, my friend. I'm the only one who sees this part of him. He swallows hard. "Lars agreed to share with my lawyer—our lawyer—and he brought it to the judge. It's the final nail for him, Sasha."

Lars was just a kid. Younger than I was when I started in this business. The thought of him tarnishing other young boys we might not know about sickens me so much that I push away my sandwich.

"Hey," Roman reaches over and squeezes my hand again. "Lars is okay. He wanted you to know that. He's been seeing a great therapist, and he only had a short contract with Moe. He said your courage to come forward first was why he did."

"He still had to be a victim. I was too stupid to recognize his manipulation. It all could have stopped with me."

Which is more of a hang up than what Moe actually did to me. To know others have suffered because I was a coward will hang over my head forever.

"Don't say that. Focus on the fact he's done now. You just need to give your final victim impact statement. It's closed door. No reporters or anything. Once it's done, you can move on with your life. Maybe with this Leaf guy you're into. Did you tell him?"

The mention of Leaf here in my real life away from the lodge seems misplaced. I imagine his bulky frame in my tiny apartment and a smile appears, regardless of the topic.

"He knows about Moe. I kind of spilled my guts to him one night."

"What did he do?"

"He hugged me and apologized that I didn't have anyone on my side to look out for me." Looking away at my laptop bag, I swallow. "I talked to him last night."

Roman pauses, his cup in the air on the way to his mouth. He sips before speaking.

"I know that tone. What did you do?"

Roman continues to eat his slop of a breakfast and it's always surprised me how easily this stuff can roll off him. Even when Roman learned Moe had stolen from his accounts too, while his agent, he simply took in stride.

He vowed to bury him where nowhere would ever find him, but still took it in stride. And now his ice-blue eyes bore into me as he waits.

"Nothing really, Ro. We had an amazing evening together and he..." I falter, remembering how Leaf let me do what I wanted to his body. Not because of the pleasure it gave him. That's just not who Leaf is. But for the pleasure it gave me. He held me as a priority and laid himself out for me, which was a huge gesture. Mammoth, really. It wasn't just sex, and it's been a struggle for my brain to accept that.

Until Leaf, I'd never actively participated in sex. I was always told what to do. On my knees, or facedown on the bed. It was devoid of feeling. Sometimes I didn't even feel human. And it was always one sided. As a model, I often played up my sexuality, but it was all just part of my facade. There was never a confidence in the bedroom for me.

Until Leaf gave me the courage to ask for what I wanted.

"Sasha?"

Roman snaps his fingers in front me with a knowing smile.

"Reliving an epic night?"

"More like an epic fairytale. He told me he loved me."

Roman's eyes bug out of his head.

"Whoa. That's a big deal. What did you say?"

I should have said something, but I simply couldn't.

"Nothing. I couldn't bring myself to say a word. It didn't seem real, you know? How is it possible I found someone to love me for me? Not the face. Not the famous name. Not the perks of having a model on your arm. Me. He loved me and the Sasha he got to know for the last four weeks."

"That's a good thing, babe. That's the real you."

"I just don't want Leaf to see me like this. Going to that courtroom, closed or not, will break me. Moe's the last tie to my mother, Ro. And I'm making sure he stays in prison with my statement. With him gone, it feels like Mom is too. I mean, she is, but it feels like my memories go with him. I'll be in a ball on the floor crying just like the day she died. I know I will and I don't want him to see me like that."

Roman's eyes soften as I try not to crumble. I miss Leaf. So much so that it feels like I left an important piece of myself behind. Oh wait, I did.

"Sasha, listen to me. Seeing you like that doesn't make you any less or whatever scenario you've imagined. I know you'll be thinking of your mom and it *will* be a hard day, but if he loves you... why not let him be here?"

"I won't be able to handle it if he leaves, Ro. I'm quite positive I left my heart in that lodge." The tears prick behind my eyes. "I don't know how to mesh us together. I've got a photography course and a business plan, and I need to move out of this place. The court stuff and finally setting out on my own, away from this horrid life in front of the camera. He's all... woodsy and shit." A small laugh escapes despite my sadness. "Catching fish and chopping wood, and did I tell you he makes maple syrup?"

Roman's smile flits on his lips.

"You mentioned it. What else?"

"Don't laugh."

He places a hand over his heart. "I promise."

I've been thinking about it on the plane, and since I landed.

"I liked being away from the city. Once the plane took off, it was like the closer I got back to here, the more my anxiety grew. And the really weird thing?" I can't believe I'm admitting this out loud. "I could see myself liking it there. Long-term."

Roman stands to clean up the take out containers. After tidying things, he leans against the sink and crosses his arms over his still apron covered torso. My best friend, my rock, lets his guard down. He blinks and swallows before looking up to the ceiling.

"Just in case it's on your mind, I know we talked about working together. You helping me with the photography part of my business... I'd follow you, Sasha. I don't need to be in a city. I can be anywhere. So if that's holding you back, don't let it. Because you're my diamond in this life and if you think you've found the one who makes you believe in yourself, I don't want you to lose that."

"Ro... god."

Stepping over to him, I wrap my arms around him and hug him so tight it hurts to breathe. We've been through a lot together and to hear him say he'd follow me so I can be happy in love? I almost can't process it.

Is it possible that something I never thought I'd have is finally within reach?

Rolling my neck, I push back from the computer screen.

After Roman left with a promise to drop by tonight, I occupied myself with cleaning up my email. Most of the messages were agents contacting me. It seems when you leave the modelling game at the top, people are even more pressed to get you to do business with them.

But I meant it when I left for good.

When I attended a rodeo last year as a favour to a friend, I learned a lot about life and myself. A group of strangers became friends. One even gave me the courage to break the cycle I was in.

And it's him I want to talk to now.

Putting it on speakerphone, I hit call. When Zane's voice answers, it's like a comforting blanket on a chilly night.

"Hey, Sash! Are you back from the mountains? No bear mauling?"

He snort laughs and I shake my head.

"Dork. Stop talking to Roman about bears. Yes, I'm back and it was amazing. I did all kinds of stuff. Outdoorsy stuff!"

"Ohhh, good for you. So are you back to the grind now? Did you make some plans while you were gone?"

"Sort of? I mean... maybe. There's been a complication."

It's hard to rattle Zane, but even over the speaker, I feel his concern.

"Oh?"

"Of the male kind."

"Oh! So spill! What happened? How did you even meet someone? I thought this was a secluded retreat kind of place?"

"Well... he owns the place. And... yeah."

There's a commotion in the background, and Zane covers the phone. His muffled voice barks out and he returns to the line. This time with complete silence.

"Sorry. The guys just started arguing over whose turn it was to go look for Matts. Since we all know it's highly likely he and Jacob are half naked somewhere, it turned into an argument."

I remember Zane telling me his friend has a thing for lavender. Whenever it's blooming in the gardens, it's like a bizarre aphrodisiac. There've been several awkward situations. Zane now carries a bell with him.

"Why do you have to look for him, then? Just wait for him to come back."

"That would be ideal, but we need to tell him today's tour with the quilting guild was moved ahead. There's some real panic happening right now. But it's not my turn to be on the search, thank god. So, tell me about this complicated man that has my friend calling me."

"He's not complicated at all. He's sweet, Zane. It's like he's so kind it's almost hard to believe he's real."

"So what's the problem, Sash? You called for a reason."

Chuckling softly, I shake my head. Zane has always been straight to the point since we became friends. I know he'll be blunt and I know he'll also care. Not that Roman doesn't care, but he's closer to me than anyone. Zane tends our friendship like the violets of his husband's, with care and a delicate touch. He weeds gently.

"So, I like him. A lot. Like I could see myself living in the woods with him kind of a lot." Sucking in a breath, I barrel on. "And the court stuff with Moe will be over this week. I have the college course and business plan almost ironed out."

"So what is it that's holding you back? I hope you're not still stuck on believing you don't deserve happiness. You have an entire friend group that love you. We know you're not just a man who loves to dress in glitter and pink sequins. That you're amazing, just as you are. And fierce as fuck, Sasha.

Don't forget how you handled yourself after being thrown from a mechanical bull. Or riding a horse that ran faster than any of us expected your second time out. I admire your spirit and courage. You're an incredible person. Sounds like this mountain man knows that, too."

"That's why I called you, Zane. Roman is good to me and he's known me longer than anyone. You and me are still new to each other and you always make me feel like I'm your closest friend."

"That's because you are a close friend. All my friends are the best ones because I only surround myself with people who are good. The people I know I can call if I need bail money or to hide a body. You're one of those people for me, Sasha. And me for you. Do you want me to be really honest?"

"As long as it doesn't make me cry, yes."

"Sasha, do not let one hideous member of the human race define who you are. You made one mistake, and it was only because you were young and didn't know. You were lost and trusted him because your mother did. That's understandable. You're not stupid and you're sure as hell not worthless. And if this man you met at the lodge is still on your mind and you connected... go to him. Hold on as tight as you did when we taught you how to hold on while the horse ran."

I bark a laugh as I remember how terrified I was that I'd fall off and break more bones. But it was the most incredible experience. My heart soared, and I laughed with pure terror, but also with delight. I felt free and invincible. Maybe that's how I can feel with Leaf.

"You're a wise man, Zane."

He snorts a laugh. "Alec will strongly disagree with you. But thank you. Did I help?"

"You did. You really did. I think I know what I'm going to do."

"Make sure you keep me posted. Am I still helping you move next month?"

"Yes! I'll keep you posted and I do still need a hand. I'd like to see you again, too."

"I'll be there, Sasha. Good luck and let me know how it goes. He's a lucky man."

"Thanks, Z. I'll let you get back to work. I hope you don't see something you shouldn't."

He groans with a chuckle.

"Me too, friend. We'll chat soon."

After ending the call, I stare at Leaf's contact in my phone. He's been quiet since our first conversation and his bumbled attempts at texting. I know he's likely swamped with things at the lodge.

Why would he be putting me first when work demands his time? I understand how it goes. But Zane is right. If I shy away from whatever this is with Leaf... then Moe still wins.

Before I can chicken out, I send him a single text.

Sasha: I miss you. Call me when you're free?

After a few minutes, when the message still sits unread, I do my best to push it out of my brain.

Turning back to my laptop, I refocus on what I hope will be something Leaf sees a future in like I do.

Chapter 21
Leaf

"Who the hell sells a cell phone without a charger!?"

Frustrated, I throw the packaging on the sofa and stare at my dead cell phone. This is why I hate technology. It always lets you down. And now I need to drive into town and get one before the store closes.

What if Sasha was trying to reach me? He probably thinks I'm ignoring him if he has.

Checking for my wallet, I then take the stairs down two at time and enter the lodge kitchen.

"Hey, Millie? I have to run into town. Is there anything we need here?"

"I don't think so. I just sent Pete yesterday. Is everything okay?"

"Yeah. Why?"

"You're all flustered and seem... unsettled."

"I need a phone charger and I just want to get to the store, so I'm not waiting longer than I have to."

"Waiting for what, exactly?"

With a huff, I look her in the eye. "I don't want Sasha to think I'm ignoring him. He might have texted or left messages and I've not returned them. What if he thinks I'm a giant asshole now?"

Millie's eyes grow wide. "He won't, love. He probably just thinks you're busy. Which you have been."

"I'm never too busy for him."

Even I shock myself at the conviction in my words.

"Then you best get to the store, Leaf. Drive safely."

Kissing the top of her head before leaving, I rush outside and slam straight into Perry.

"Oof. Where's the fire, bro?"

"I need a phone charger. There wasn't one in my box."

"Cool. Can I come with?"

He doesn't wait for my answer and just slides into the passenger seat.

"What are you still doing here, anyway? I thought you had plans for tonight and were leaving before supper?"

"Yeah, I did. They backed out. So you're stuck with me."

He flashes me a smile and I laugh as I drive us off the lodge property.

"I guess it's my lucky night, then. You're a good guy to be stuck with."

He hums under his breath and I glance his way.

"What?"

"Have you talked to Sasha?"

"Just once. It's mostly been text. That's why I'm running for a charger. I'm so stupid. It never occurred to me I'd need to plug the damn thing in. I don't know how long it's been dead, but he might have tried to call me."

I feel the hysteria building in my voice, and I have to force myself to take a calming breath.

"It happens, Leaf. Don't sweat it. He knows you're new to the technology of the modern world."

"You make me sound like a dinosaur." I grumble and he laughs with glee.

"But seriously, have you thought about him? Like, actually going after him or anything?"

"I can't just go after him. He has things in his life to deal with and he asked for space. I'm doing what he asked me to."

The silence in the cab makes me sweat. Perry isn't a love expert, but he's got far more love experience than I do, even if they never turned into long-term relationships. But he loves hard on all the people in his life and I've trusted him before.

He did, after all, convince me Connor was worth it. Then moved here so we could stay close.

I hope I don't regret this.

"Okay, Perry. What is it I should do exactly?"

"Didn't you read any of those romance books he likes? You must have got some ideas?"

The day Sasha left, housekeeping brought me the two novels I'd seen him reading. He left them behind with a note saying to pass on to anyone who loves to read romance. They brought them to me and while I'm not a huge reader, I skimmed them. I also paid attention to the pages Sasha dog-eared.

But as romantic as the stories were, that's all they were to me.

"They're just stories, Perry."

He clucks his tongue.

"God, you're thick. Sasha loves them. He loves romance, and you even said the books he reads are very romantic."

"There's romance and then there's being real, Perry. I don't have a yacht for romantic dinners in the Mediterranean. There's no lush Florida landscape here with tropical flowers and paradise. It's just acres of maple trees and wilderness. A lake and a shitload of mosquitoes. I'm not sure how that can be romantic."

Arriving at the store I bought the phone from, I'm relieved to see the open sign still flashing.

"You forgot one thing."

"Yeah, a charger."

"Would you shut up for a minute? He didn't leave those books behind for anyone. And he took the time to make you that photo book thing."

"Okay?"

Perry heaves a dramatic sigh. "For god's sake, Leaf, be fucking romantic. Woo the man. He deserves it."

"Can we talk about this after I get my charger? Because there won't be any of this wooing you speak of if I can't get in touch with him."

Perry sighs and gets out, following me into the mobile store where I barely contain my anger at the salesperson's attitude.

"My brother still lights a candle to go to the outhouse. Cut him slack. And give him what he needs to have a charger in his truck, too. He'll need a lighter attachment because he also hasn't updated his vehicle in ninety years."

The clerk examines my phone, and I shoot daggers at my brother. He only grins back.

"You're a jerk, you know that?"

"I've been called worse. But I got you what you need and I'll show you what to do. You can check in on your *amour* as soon as we get in the truck."

Walking back to the truck with a much lighter wallet, Perry opens the packages and sets up my charger.

"It will take a few minutes for it to have enough juice to pick up the signal and notify you of the missed messages. But back to what we were talking about earlier. Be honest, if Sasha hadn't said he needed space or whatever, what would you be doing right now?"

Perry sets my phone, now connected to a charger and showing the very red, and very drained, battery signal, in my cup holder.

"I'd probably be calling him and if he lived closer, asking him on a date. Maybe take him to the city to that big book store. And he loves clothes, so I'd offer to go to the outlet place. You know the one Millie says her daughters buy all the fancy purses at? I'd take him there. We'd get ice cream at the creamery and he might like a walk along the riverfront."

I abruptly stop my word vomit and look at Perry.

"I didn't realize I'd thought about it so much. What does that mean?"

"Maybe that you want him in your life and you're ready to make it happen." He shrugs. "Or maybe you're just obsessed."

My phone buzzes. One after another of missed texts pop up. Perry stops my hand when I reach for it.

"Just let it keep going for a minute and look at me."

The soft tone of his voice draws my full attention to my normally brash and in your face little brother.

"I don't want to pry or upset you. I told you how I felt when we took Sasha out. You were back. The Leaf I know and love is back. You've even been back at the sugar shack this week. But I want to make sure you understand what Sasha said. Are you sure he wants you to stay away, and it's not just him hoping for romance? Maybe wishing you'd show up on his doorstep with flowers or something?"

"He's spent his whole life being told what to do, Perry. Not as a child, as an adult. He was taken advantage of and... used. There's no other way to say it. He has such a distorted sense of himself and reality. Sasha came here to find his independence and to just... try to be normal. Do things of his choosing."

I smile, remembering how excited he was to chop a piece of wood. Something I've done my whole life without considering if it was okay or if I was allowed to do it.

"And I don't want to share many details, but I know there were issues in the bedroom with others. Like... I think the men he was with just treated him as something to fuck. They didn't see him as a person or really make him feel cared for. It's hard for him to let people in."

Perry nods with a sad smile.

"I'm sorry. That's a shitty way to feel. So you don't want to overstep then? Is that it?"

"As much as I want to run to him and tell him we need to give us a shot, I can't go to him when he asked me not to, Perry. That's not listening or caring about his voice and he's had too much of that."

He gestures to the cell phone. "You want to call him and I'll take a walk so you can have privacy?"

"No. I'll send him a text right now and call him at home."

Perry accepts that and leans back as I scroll through all the texts from Sasha before sending one to say I'd be calling shortly. But before I can text, I stop and read the last message.

> **Beauty:** I miss you. Call me when you're free?

I'm probably jumping to conclusions about what it means, but I hastily reply and spin my tires before leaving the parking lot.

"Must have been a good text." Perry chuckles.

"It was, and I dare to hope it means there's more to come. In the meantime, tell me how I can be romantic when he's six hours away from me."

Perry sits up and rubs his hands together.

"I'm so glad you asked. I have ideas."

And for the next twenty minutes, my brother tells me lots of ideas.

And they're actually pretty good.

Chapter 22
Sasha

I'm just crawling into bed with a book when my phone rings with Leaf's ringtone. I don't think it's even finished one full ring before I'm rushing to answer it.

"Hey, Leaf."

"Sasha, I'm so sorry it took me so long to call. My phone died, and I didn't have a charger. Then I got back, and some lodgers roped me into their after dinner card game and fish talk. Millie needed me to move some stuff into the kitchen and... yeah. I'm sorry."

Leaf's voice edges on panic and I find it endearing that he's so concerned about my feelings.

"You don't need to be sorry. I'm happy you called. Things happen."

A breath of relief over the line is clear as a bell and I fucking miss him. So much.

"Fuck, it's good to hear your voice. I miss you."

Placing the phone on the pillow next to me, I put the call on speaker and pretend he's laying there with me.

"Me too. Do you have time to talk now for a while? I... I've made some decisions and I want to know what you think."

"My phone has a full battery and I'm in for the night. You have me for as much time as you want."

His voice is soft and I picture him reclining on the sunset loveseat. Maybe with his nighttime tea nearby.

"Are you sitting near the window in your favourite spot?"

"I am. No sun, though. Just the moon over the water. It's still pretty."

I release a slow breath. "How would you feel having company on that seat?"

He sucks in a sharp breath and I curl my hands into the comforter while I wait for his answer.

"There's only one person I'd like to share this space with. And if it's who I hope you mean, my response is I'd love it more than anything, and how soon?"

I gasp. Relieved and swamped with emotion that Leaf truly wants me there. And I struggle to control my tears and emotions so I can talk.

"I've been thinking a lot and I have a plan. To ah, make a change. Live a happy life. And if you want me there, I have a huge ask of you."

Leaf's answering voice is thick with emotion. It warms my heart to hear that he's as moved as I am with whatever this is we have growing between us.

"Somehow I don't think whatever it is you ask of me will be much Sasha."

Smiling at how easy everything seems to Leaf, I tell him about my photography space and how I found a place in the town of Maple to serve as a studio. How my course work can be completed mostly online. Except for the gallery event near the end, I don't need to attend everything in person.

"So you can come here to stay? With me?"

His voice cracks and I find the smile staying on my face longer.

"I can look for an apartment if you prefer. I know it's rather soon to —"

"No. I want you with me every morning, Sasha. I don't care what people think. That's not a huge ask at all, baby. I just wish you'd be here tomorrow."

God. This man. How did I get so lucky?

"Well, that's not actually my ask. But I'm delighted to hear how excited you are to have my clothes all over your space."

His throaty laugh sends goosebumps racing down my body.

"And on the floor. On the sofa. You look great without them... just sayin'." He schools his voice. "Really Sasha, just knowing you're willing to come back means everything to me."

"How did I find someone as good as you?"

I swallow, blinking the fresh pricks of tears back. Thank fuck Roman talked sense into me about this man and I didn't run completely.

"I could say the same thing." Leaf murmurs. "Tell me what else you need. I'll make it happen."

"So, my best friend Roman, I told you about him. The one that's just getting started designing lingerie?"

"Yes, I remember. He thinks I'm a hot lumberjack. Same guy, right?"

"Yes," I laugh. "That's him. Anyway, he's part of my business plan. We don't have any official contracts in place, but... he wants to follow me, Leaf."

"Okay? And what do you need me to do?"

Nothing weird about asking the man you only just fell for to help your best friend who plans to follow you while you follow your heart.

"I was hoping you'd let him stay at the lodge. He'd pay, of course, but he's a social person and I don't want him staying in a new town by himself. I want to keep him close to me. We'd be more efficient, and I'd be closer to you, too."

There's a pause while I hold my breath.

"I'll have to check the bookings, but I think we can make it happen once the summer is over. There's a family suite that doesn't get booked as often, so he'd have more space there. If he likes it, we can look at a long-term contract or move him to one of the cabins. Oh! What about the cabin on the sugar bush? We could always modernize it and he could stay there. Or it could be your studio!"

Leaf's enthusiasm leaves me breathless. He keeps rattling off solutions to house Roman and make our business venture more profitable. He's talking so fast with so many possibilities, all for me. I don't really know what to say, except how I feel.

"I love you," I whisper, and Leaf falls silent.

"What?" His voice, full of disbelief and hope, has me spew out everything I should have said to his face before I left.

"I love you. I love how you make me feel and talk to me like I'm a real person. I love how you never laugh at any of the stupid things I say when I clearly should know better. I love how you respect my wishes asking for space and I love that you make maple syrup like it's no big deal when I think it's the most amazing thing a person could make." Closing my eyes, I picture Leaf in his living room, perhaps shirtless as he has his nightly tea or whiskey neat. "And I love that you have room for me in your life and your heart."

"Sasha..."

"I'm sorry that I couldn't say that to you in person before I left. I was scared, and I needed time to process everything I had swirling around in my head. But I promise it's the first thing I'm going to say to you when I see you next."

His voice is gruff with emotion. "When can I see you?"

"Are you free to come here? I think... no, I know, I'll need someone after this court thing on Friday. I understand you can't just take off, but if you could be here, I think I'd like that."

"I'll be there as soon as I can. When is your meeting?"

"Friday afternoon. 2 P.M.. Roman will be with me and it's a closed door meeting. You can't come in."

"Oh, baby, I'm so sorry you have to do this."

And I know he means it. Not with pity, like I'm used to. But because he doesn't want to see me hurt. If Leaf could wave a wand and make it all go away I know he would.

"Me too. But it'll be better knowing you'll be waiting."

I stifle a yawn and stare at the phone, wishing I could turn it into a real-life Leaf. I so badly want him to hold me and reassure me in person. To feel his strong arms around me and have his beard against my cheek.

"You need some sleep and I need to make some travel plans. Can you send me your address and anything else I should know before you get your rest?"

"I suppose you need that if you want to find me." I laugh softly. "Thank you, Leaf. I'll send you a text before I turn out the light."

"I love you, *mon amour*. I'd wander the earth to find you, but an address would make it easier."

My heart feels like it's too big for my chest and after several more whispers of promises and love, I finally end the call with a new hope simmering.

And a lumberjack booking a flight to me.

The days have passed in a blur, and I can't believe Friday is already here. The day to face Moe one final time.

Even though I know he's going to jail and this is for sentencing, my guts have churned all morning and I've kept nothing down. Roman always wears his armour for both of us, but I notice the dark circles under his eyes and concern when he glances my way.

My phone buzzes with a text, and my one slice of silver on this otherwise dark day pops up.

> **Leaf:** I'm finally boarding. I'll get to you as quick as I can. Remember, you're strong and people love you. I love you.

"Is that Leaf?"

"Yeah, his plane was late leaving and this will be over by the time he gets here."

"I'm really proud of you for telling him how you feel. He sounds like a great guy. I can't wait to meet him."

Our taxi pulls up in front of the courthouse and my stomach does another somersault. Roman pays the driver and as he drives away, I stand frozen in front of the giant stone building.

"Is your lawyer here already?"

"*Our* lawyer, Sasha. Yes, he said he'd meet us in the hall outside courtroom C."

My feet move like giant blocks of concrete, heavy and loud. Sapping all my energy just to enter the building.

Roman takes my hand, his grip tight, and he bumps our shoulders together.

"We'll get through this. Believe in us, okay?"

Nodding, I let Roman lead me and once inside, the halls suffocate me. Both of us wear conservative suits, although Roman refused to not wear his trademark business corset. He said he wanted Moe to see him as a force and not a boy he could take advantage of. Roman wasn't dressing down for someone in the wrong, and he was proud of who he was.

I didn't want to draw any attention to myself. I'd camouflage into the carpet if I could. It already felt like I was a beacon with the number of looks we got when people walked by. Part of the price you pay for having a somewhat famous face.

"Roman. Sasha. I have a room for us to wait in so you can be more comfortable."

"Thanks, Morgan."

Morgan has been Roman's lawyer since he started modelling when we were just kids. He's been like the dad neither of us ever had. When he offered to take this on for me as well as Roman, I couldn't have been more grateful. I was completely useless with this stuff. Moe kept me sheltered from the world as much as he could when I first became somewhat famous.

He kept me with him all the time and monitored my internet use and even what news I read. He censored my entire life.

I trusted him and never questioned it. He was my mother's friend, and she'd never let anyone harm me. Which is why today is more difficult than anything I've ever done. Mom would be crushed if she knew how he wronged both of us.

"You look a little pale, Sasha. Would you like some water before I give you the rundown on what will happen?"

Morgan gently squeezes my shoulder as I ease into a chair.

"Please. Thank you for this."

"I wish we met under different circumstances." He places water in front of Roman and me before sitting at the end of the small table.

"Let me tell you what will happen and what you should say once we're in there."

Morgan explains to us how Moe will arrive and where he'll sit. What the judge will ask me and possibly what Moe's lawyer will ask if he does. But today is a formality, mostly. He's going to prison for a long time. Morgan wanted me to give a victim impact statement to be sure the judge knew the severity of Moe's actions. He'd prepared it along with one for Roman and all I had to do was read it.

Sounds easy, but with Moe a few steps away, I know I'll be stammering like a fool.

"Just read off the paper, Sasha. This should all be over in thirty minutes or less."

"And I don't have to do this ever again, right? It's done?"

"It's done."

And I can finally begin to heal.

Another slice of silver on this shitty day.

Chapter 23
Leaf

Why the hell does everything happen slow when you're in a hurry?

My flight arrived late, now I'm stuck in traffic. When I chose a driving service instead of a rental, part of the hope was that it would get me to Sasha faster. So badly I wanted him to find me outside the courthouse, waiting. Because of my late arrival, I'm going straight to his place now. But this traffic stoppage is bullshit.

After texting when I landed, he'd acknowledged the message with a heart. Normally that wouldn't worry me, but he's been so quiet for the past two days. I need to hold him and see for myself that he hasn't retreated further into himself. For the rest of my life, I'll tell him how amazing he is every day and I want to start now. No, I wanted to start two weeks ago.

"Any idea how much longer we have to go?"

The driver catches my gaze in the rearview mirror.

"Do you want that in distance or time?"

"Both."

"It's downtown traffic. Commuters start early to head home. Driving we're at least twenty minutes, maybe more, because there's a construction zone ahead. How well do you know the city?"

He reaches for his phone and taps while I answer.

"I don't. It's my first time."

"If you want to walk, I'll draw you a map and you'll probably get there faster."

"Really? It's safe where you'll send me?"

Not that I'm afraid for my safety, but I don't need to risk an injury when Sasha needs me.

"Yep. High end residential neighbourhood and you'll cut through a small park. Probably take ten minutes. And you can work off some of that nervous energy instead of sitting here."

His smile is knowing, and I nod in agreement.

"If you don't mind, I'd appreciate it and I'll pay full fare for the help. You're right. I feel like I might just run all the way there. I need to get out of this car."

Still smiling, he rips a piece of paper off a notepad next to him and hands it to me. "It's super easy to get there. Cut through Tulip Park, there are signs. Look for Orchid Way on the other side and it should be halfway down the street. It's probably a stone house and sometimes the numbers are hard to see. Good luck."

I'd only packed a small backpack and carried it on with me. After paying the man, I jump out with map in hand and throw the pack on my back. After carefully darting across four lanes of traffic, I jog toward the sign for Tulip Park.

The park is gorgeous. A fountain, an outdoor pop-up cafe, and loads of flower beds. Maybe I'll have Sasha take me here later. Checking my little map, I turn left and look for Orchid Way. It's two blocks from the park and after waiting at a crosswalk for what feels like an eternity, I'm finally walking down Sasha's street.

It feels like six hours passed and not six minutes until I find his house. The driver was right. It's a large stone house with several entrances. Sasha said he lived in a studio apartment, but I don't know what floor.

Hitting call on his number in my cell, I stand in the driveway and wait. An unfamiliar voice answers the phone.

"Um... hi? I'm looking for Sasha."

"Is this Leaf?"

"Yeah, is he okay?"

"He is. Where are you?"

"I'm in the driveway and I don't know what entrance to use."

"Go around to the back. I'll let you in."

Jogging down the driveway, my heart now racing, I turn the corner to the back of the building. As I round the corner, a stunning young man holds a door open for me. His eyes are the bluest shade I've ever seen, like a clear sky on the sunniest day, and the corset is a giveaway.

"Are you Roman?"

He smiles a cocky smile and holds out his hand. "You must be Leaf."

We shake and he motions me inside. A small staircase leads up to another door, and before I can race up them, he grabs my arm.

"Thank you for coming when he asked. I know he shared a lot of crap about today with you and he doesn't tell many people about that."

"I'd do anything he asked me to, Roman. When I care about someone, I move mountains to help them when they ask. There's no in between with me."

Roman's eyes widen at my statement, and I squeeze his shoulder.

"I know you're close to him. That offer goes for you too. If you're Sasha's support, then I'm yours too."

Roman stands frozen in place. He blinks, disbelief clear at my words.

"Well, hell..." He sniffs and looks away. "Do you have a twin?"

He laughs, but I raise my eyebrow. "I have a younger brother."

Roman snaps his mouth shut. "Get up there to see Sasha."

Taking the stairs two at a time, I don't even knock when I reach the top. I throw the door open and my gaze immediately finds Sasha. He's at a small table in his kitchen, still in his suit with his tie hanging loose around his neck and the buttons of his shirt partly undone. A half empty glass sits in front of him.

"Sasha."

His head snaps up with a gasp. Pushing his chair back, it clatters to the floor as he runs into my arms.

"You're here." He runs his fingers through my beard with a sigh.

"I am. I've missed you. Are you okay?"

He presses his lips together and nods. Firm and... confident.

"I stared that fucker down, Leaf. And I told a room full of strangers how he took advantage of my mother's kind soul to steal from her son! Her underage son!" His lips tremble as he cups my face. "And I looked him in the eye and told him he may have stolen happy years of my life, but I still have a future ahead of me. That is something I won't let him have." His voice wavers only slightly. "He doesn't get to take anything else from me."

His newfound determination and confidence to move forward fills me with immense pride.

"I knew you could do it. You're strong. Stronger than me in a lot of ways, and it's just one thing that I love about you."

There are so many things I love about him. How he chose himself, and us, instead of collapsing. His strength will always be something I admire.

"I was supposed to tell you I love you first."

His hands slide down my arms and he puffs a breath.

"You're in my apartment. And I love you." A laugh bursts from his lips and I join him, my smile stretching across my face. My heart just about bursting from my chest.

"I am." He twines our fingers together and we stare at each other with ridiculous smiles.

"Uh, sorry, but I'm just going to grab my things and leave you two alone."

Roman gathers a messenger bag and folds his suit jacket over his arm. Sasha hugs him before he can leave and whispers in his ear. They hold each other for a long while and I'm so happy Sasha has him in his life. If Roman will follow him to Maple, they have a bond to be nurtured just as much as ours.

He nods as he passes by. "Be good to him, Leaf. He's a treasure."

The door clicks behind him, and Sasha chews on his lip before stepping back to me.

"Leaf... do we need to go anywhere for the next few hours?"

His fingers dance over the buttons on my shirt and I shake my head slowly.

"The only place I want to be is here. With you. Right now."

"Good." he breathes as I drop my pack to the floor and pull him to me.

Crashing my mouth over his, Sasha's hands curl into my shoulders as he moulds himself to my body. Infusing himself to me.

"I want you to get naked. Then I'm going to lick every inch of your body and show you how fucking happy I am to see you." He pants as we grab at each other's clothes.

We're a frenzy of hands and kisses as we stumble our way to the bed in the corner. His apartment is a true studio, with his bedroom in the corner and living room across from it. The only separate room is the bathroom, but I don't care right now. I'm focused on getting this man into bed. Or whatever surface he wants. I'm not picky.

The backs of my legs meet the edge of the mattress and Sasha pushes me back with unexpected force. He tears my pants down my legs in record time and snaps at the elastic band of my boxers.

"You're so damn hot, Leaf." his eyes rake over me as I pant beneath him. I love snuggly, tender Sasha. But this version? The boldness and shameless want? Yep. Sign me up.

"How hot?" My lips twitch when he pauses, considering my question. He's actually thinking about a reply.

Sliding his fingers into my waistband, he now has me completely naked, and he taps a finger against his lips in thought.

"Hotter than the sun? Is that hot enough?"

"Be careful. My ego might get too inflated."

"It's not your ego I want inflated."

He winks, and I bark a laugh as he sheds his remaining clothes. He's so wild and uninhibited. Not at all like the Sasha I had in my bed last. There's no hesitation or shyness. He's bold and going for what he wants and I. AM. HERE. FOR. IT.

"Tell me what you want, my beauty."

Because that's what he is. A beautiful soul, mind, and body. And he's mine until the earth takes him away from me.

He falters, his playful grin softening as he cups my cheek with a tender hand.

"I like that name, beauty. *Your* beauty. From you, it means something different. Not just my face on a page, but you see all of me."

Sasha swallows, the charge between us still crackling, before he drops a soft kiss to my lips.

With the tender moment passed, he crawls on top of me, nestling himself over my cock with a gentle rock of his hips. His lips turn up in a troublemaking grin and even though he's teasing the fuck out of me, I love it. I love everything about this.

"I want you to suck me." He crawls up on his knees and hovers over my mouth, sliding his cock across my lips. "And I want to come down your throat. Will you do that?"

I open my mouth in response, and his eyes are liquid pools of fire.

He feeds his cock past my lips, one hand fisted into my hair. His chest heaves and his eyes widen, like he can't believe my lips are wrapped around his dick.

With tentative thrusts, he fucks my mouth. Sometimes moving my head and other times rocking his hips. If I gag—and I do—he pauses, lips parted with shaky breaths.

And for every second that passes, I love him just a bit more. I'm the one he trusts to have all these experiences with.

Balls slap my chin, and he moans. Guttural. Uninhibited and sexy as hell.

He empties his load down my throat with a surprised gasp and pulls out of my mouth before he finishes. Cum splashes on my face and, with his entire body shaking, he slides down to lie next to me and feathers the sweetest kiss on my swollen lips.

"I'm sorry I didn't warn you. It just sort of hit me."

"It's okay." His hands wipe the stray splashes from my face and I catch his wrist. Placing a soft kiss on it, I tug him over on top of me.

He still trembles and I'm not sure if it's because of his orgasm or something else. Something more profound than his confidence in the bedroom shifted within him today.

"Do you want to get all this showered off?"

Sasha shakes his head and scrunches his eyebrows together.

"No. I want to ride this." He reaches back to squeeze my dick. "I want you to scream my name and beg me to stop."

"Jesus..."

"No, he's not here. But I bet I can take you to see his dad."

I laugh at his playfulness. His sex-filled smirk is everything.

"Are there neighbours we need to be concerned with hearing all this?"

He shrugs and reaches for the lube. "Who cares?"

I'd laugh if he didn't already have his slippery hand around my cock. He's intent on watching my reaction to everything he does. While he touches and kisses everywhere with confidence, his eyes carry a soft worry. Almost like he doesn't want me to be displeased with a single thing. And I want to make it my mission for him to never doubt his actions in or out of the bedroom about who he is. Or what he means to me.

"I want you up here, beauty. Actually, can we change spots?"

"As long as I still have your dick in me, we can go anywhere."

Shaking my head as I sit and swing myself off his bed, I double check for what I saw earlier and smile.

There's a padded bench at the end of the bed that will work perfectly.

"Get your fine ass over here and sit on my lap like you promised."

With a squeak that's reminiscent of a *Muppet*, he scrambles off the bed to join me. I've lounged back, legs spread, and hold my hard cock for him. "Make yourself comfortable."

With a lick of his lips, he kneels over me and lowers himself slowly. Sasha stares into my face, incredulous, before testing how it feels to move. We both groan. He does it again and bites his lip.

"Shit, Leaf... this is... incredible."

A rosy glow forms on his cheeks as he rocks on my dick. Sweat shines on his forehead and he's the most beautiful man in the world. And he's mine. "So are you. Don't stop."

He finds a rhythm, bracing his hands on my chest, and sets his own pace. Sliding a hand through his hair, I pull him down to my mouth. In between kisses, I whisper on soft breaths how fucking amazing he is. How I'm looking forward to building something with him. A new life. A new future. How incredibly gone for him I am.

Everything I thought I'd lost is now found again, and I don't think he knows how much it means to me. To have my heart follow another after all these years feels like I get a second chance at living again. A new purpose.

"I'm gonna come again." He throws his head back as he coats my stomach with his release. Completely spent, he sags against me.

Gripping his hips in place, I come with his name on my lips and a groan sure to be heard through the walls, just like he wanted.

Panting and boneless, he rests his forehead on mine.

"Thank you." He whispers with a soft kiss. "I can't put into words what having you here means to me. And this, this was more than just a fuck. This was something more and I think you know that."

I rub my nose along his.

"I do. I don't want to see the worry in your eyes. Never with me. If you want something from me, say the word. I will never make you feel like less and I'll certainly never use you." I kiss him again, revelling in the tender moment and all we've been through to get here.

"I know you won't. Be patient if I sometimes forget, though? Brains are a tricky thing."

He rests his head against my shoulder with a small huff, and I kiss his neck.

"Of course. And you'll be just as patient with me if I slip back to my old ways."

Easing himself off my cock, I watch a trail of cum run down the inside of his thigh. He follows my gaze and laughs softly.

"So, about that shower?"

"Is there room for two?"

"It's the best thing about this apartment. There's room for at least three."

He winks and offers his hand when I scowl.

Placing a kiss on my chest, he peers up at me.

"Don't worry. That's something I'm not wired to do. One-on-one is all I can handle."

He pulls me with him towards the bathroom.

"Unless toys count as a third? I'd do that."

Barking a laugh, I shake my head. From shy and unsure to blazing full of confidence and offering sex toys, so much has changed since we first met.

And something tells me my life from now on will never be dull.

Chapter 24
Sasha

"Four days isn't long enough. I miss you already."

Leaf and I stroll hand in hand through Tulip Park near my apartment. It's been three and a half days of self-discovery and opening ourselves to each other like I've never done before.

And sex. So. Much. Sex.

Which most people would expect with a new couple. As someone with an issue of being used purely for my looks and body, I never trust people's intentions. This has been a massive shift for me. It doesn't come easy. But with Leaf, he makes me feel safe. No matter what he says and does, I know he respects every part of me.

It's not perfect. There are still a lot of mountains for me to climb yet in order to address all my past issues, but the important part is I know he truly supports me.

"I know. I can't wait until you get things sorted and come to me. I'll make time to get here again if it will be too long." His voice is laced with sadness but also excitement for the future. "We haven't talked about the logistics much either."

"You said you slow down at the end of October, right? Then it's quiet for the winter?"

He nods and stops in the middle of the park path. Snaking an arm around my waist, he pulls me close and kisses me. Deep and slow and it makes me dizzy. Like I spent too much time in the darkroom and my legs wobble. Leaf holds me tighter.

"What was that for?" I breathe.

"What I hope to do through the winter."

"Oh."

If the promise of Leaf kissing me like that all the time doesn't scramble my brain, I don't know what will. That's a definite incentive to get all my ducks in a row and get there for the winter. Or sooner.

"I like it when I can render you speechless."

Leaf laughs and I peer up at his smiling face. The sun picks up a bit of red in his beard. The laugh lines at the edge of his eyes deepen as he smiles at me, and for a moment I wonder how we even got here. Two broken people with so many fractures... there was a time that I felt beyond repair.

He's achingly handsome and I can't wait for us to start a life together. Even while teasing me when he knows I'm a full on chatterbox, I wouldn't want it any other way.

"Don't get so cocky. I'm not opposed to your plans. At all." I kiss him quickly and step out of his arms. "I just thought there might be something else you do in your downtime. Like... I don't know, pose for lumberjack calendars or bake cookies.

Save kittens from trees." I wave my hand in the air. "You know, stuff."

With a snort, he takes my hand as we leave the park on the way to my favourite Thai restaurant. I'll definitely miss that place once I leave. Their spring rolls are to die for.

"Do you want to make a calendar of me for your final project? All you need to do is ask, you know."

"Huh. I didn't even think of that. Would you?"

"Would I what? Be specific, beauty."

He opens the door for me at the restaurant where our take out order should be ready. My stomach rumbles and I wonder when we last ate a full meal.

"Okay. Would you be willing to do a lumberjack calendar for my project? It might involve baking."

He boops a finger on my nose and I must look like a complete fool with the ridiculous smile on my face.

"I'd love to."

"Mr. Sasha! So nice to see you. Who's your friend?"

The owner of the restaurant rushes out and wraps me in a hug. She's a tiny thing, all four feet of her, but her personality is huge.

"Hi, Candy. This is Leaf. I'm introducing him to your spring rolls tonight."

She shakes Leaf's hand after she releases me and pushes the bill across the counter. I swat Leaf's hand away when he reaches for it and pass her my credit card.

"It's my treat. Don't argue."

Leaf pushes his hands in his pockets with a sigh and Candy chuckles.

"It's nice to see you smiling, Mr. Sasha. He's handsome. You're keeping him?"

My laughter is loud, and Leaf bites back a smile. She calls me Mr. Sasha because she thinks it's my last name and I just couldn't bring myself to correct her. Plus, I think it's cute.

"He's definitely a keeper. So much so that I'll be moving away with him. I'll miss seeing you, Candy."

"Ah... love is bigger than spring rolls, right? I'm happy for you. But I'll miss seeing you, too."

She comes around the counter again and hugs me a second time, taking me off guard. Hugging her back with a lump in my throat, I catch Leaf's soft gaze watching us.

"Enjoy the food and maybe bring him back for a visit sometime. Best wishes, Mr. Sasha."

Leaf agrees he'd love to visit and takes our bag, ushering me outside, all the time wishing her well and other thoughtful things that I can't hear because I zoned out.

"Hey, you okay?"

Huffing a breath, I take Leaf's hand as we walk back toward my apartment.

"I wasn't prepared to hear a random lady tell me she'll miss me, then hug me. I didn't think she cared that much."

"She's not random, Sasha. You obviously see her a lot and made an impression. There are people in this world who see you for the light that you are, Sasha. I know it's hard, but remember that."

"I'll try."

He kisses me on the cheek. "That's all I can ask."

It's all I can give. I make no promises because I know the journey will be a hard one.

But I'm working on it.

"Why am I doing this again? Someone remind me, please?"

I'm not built for heavy manual labour.

Roman grunts as he juggles his end of the table and we finally exit the apartment.

"Because you're in love and it's gross?"

"That sounds like someone who hasn't found the right one yet," Zane quips as he helps settle the table in the *U-Haul*. Roman throws an evil look his way.

"I'm perfectly happy, thank you. And don't start spouting about soulmates and love and that crap. It's great that it's for you. I don't want it."

Zane just smiles and shrugs. Perfectly content and full of sunshine, no matter what gets tossed his way.

"Okay. Suit yourself." Roman seems shocked at Zane's dismissal, but Zane is never one to argue. "How much more has to come down?"

"Mostly my personal stuff that's coming with me to Leaf's. But that all stays at Roman's until he joins me in the spring. So... we might be done?"

Hopping out of the truck, Zane secures the doors. "Let's all go up and take a final look then. We can put all the boxes in Roman's car and call it a day."

It's hard to believe almost a month has passed since Leaf was here. So much has changed for me. The ugliness with Moe is now done and buried. He's gone to prison for a long time. When Morgan delivered the news he received a maximum sentence, I'm not ashamed to say I jumped with joy. My heart is lighter with the knowledge that no one else will be his victim. One more step on my path of healing.

My trust account funds were recovered. The money I know my mom wanted me to use to get a leg up in life. Knowing Mom, she probably wanted me to buy a nice house and put down roots. Build a picket fence and start a family. All the things we never had.

In a way, I guess that's what I'm doing. Assuming Leaf is okay with the plan I came up with.

Entering the mostly empty apartment, I puff out a breath. Roman loops his arm around my waist and I rest my head on his shoulder.

"It's hard to believe this is it, Ro. No more movie nights in bed eating licorice. No more breakfast from the diner when you know I'm sad."

"Ah, but there will be Sasha. We're only apart for a few months. Then I'm sure Leaf won't mind me in your bed with licorice." He laughs when I smack his chest. "And it's not over, it's just paused. We'll have breakfast again before you know it."

He tries to hide the crack in his voice, but I know he's sad. Even though he'll be following me soon to start our business together, it's a huge change in both our lives.

"Yeah, we will. You'll love the coffee shop, Roman. The brownies are amazing."

Zane piles boxes on the handcart and heads out, leaving Roman and I alone. If there's one thing Zane excels at, it's knowing when people need time to gather themselves. God knows he's done it with me many, many times.

"We're gonna be okay, Sasha. New direction, right?"

"Onwards and upwards, Ro. You and I will take the world by storm. With your designs and my photography, we're gonna fly."

And they're not empty words. I mean them.

For the first time in my life, I'm excited about my future and not just because it involves my best friend and the man of my dreams. They're plans *I* made. That *I* want. Nobody chose for me or forced me into this path. If I fail, it's on me. But I don't believe I will.

"Like Icarus?" He huffs.

"No. Like an eagle, Ro. With big claws and a sharp beak. We're unfuckwithable."

"Is that a real word?"

"I don't know, but I like it."

"Let's put it on jackets."

"Only if they're sparkly."

"Done."

Roman lifts one of my suitcases and, with a pat on my shoulder, he leaves me.

Taking a moment by myself in my space, I don't cry. My heart pounds with excitement at what's ahead.

My keys clatter extra loud as I set them on the counter like the landlord instructed. From my laptop bag, I pull out the thank-you card for them. They were such great people when I first moved here and needed some adult guidance.

Sometimes you find the right people at the right time in your life and the Becks were that for me. I've left my forwarding address and I know I'll keep in touch with them.

With one final glance around the place I called home for the last eight years, I close the door behind me and I don't go down the stairs with tears, but with a smile. Bursting through the back door, Zane and Roman stand waiting for me.

"You ready for the next step, Sasha?"

Zane twirls the keys to the truck around his finger as Roman leans on his car.

"To new starts and new lives. Let's rock and roll boys!"

Zane grins and pulls me into a hug.

"I'm disappointed we didn't get to spend much time together, but I understand why you're in a hurry. I'm so happy for you, Sasha."

"Thanks, Z. You'll have to bring Alec back for a visit. I'd love for you to meet Leaf. I miss you."

He laughs as he steps towards the truck.

"I bet I can get Alec back there again. You know how he loves nature and the outdoors. Let me know when you get there."

Zane starts the truck with all the furniture I own inside. I donated it all to the LGBTQ youth shelter in his town. It seemed like the right thing to do. A kid there might need a fresh start, just like I did before and like I'm doing again right now.

He pulls out, waving out the window as he drives away, leaving me and Roman in the driveway.

"Ready for the airport?" Roman opens the driver's door and I walk to the passenger side.

"I was ready a month ago."

Roman snorts. "Lovesick sap. What happened to my friend?"

"Nothing, Ro. He's still here. I just learned that sometimes in life we need to accept the gifts given."

He tilts his head with a small smile.

"Leaf gets the best one."

"Now who's the sap?"

Laughing, he puts the car in drive. "Don't you dare tell anyone I have a soft side."

With the windows down and the cool crisp fall air blowing our hair around, I grin at my best friend.

"I wouldn't dream of it."

Chapter 25
Leaf

The busy summer lodge season has ended, and fall has arrived.

So much has changed. Including me.

While I missed Sasha being away for the rest of the summer, I also looked forward to our nightly calls. We talked about everything and once Perry showed me how to use *FaceTime*, I got to see him every night.

I made those calls a priority.

The first thing I did when it was official that he'd move here was rearrange my schedule and assign duties to the staff to free up my time. I should have done it years ago, but work allowed me to forget what I lost. The distraction soon became a habit, and it was hard to change. With a second chance at living and love, I wanted Sasha to know he would always come first in my life. There was no better time to begin my own new way of life right along with Sasha.

We didn't sext every night. Sometimes we did, and it was the hottest thing on this side of the moon. But we also showed each other what we'd been doing. I rearranged the closets for him and brought in another wardrobe for his clothes. He joked I should just give him the closet and take all the drawers, since I only wear jeans and t-shirts. He makes a good point and I might consider it.

I cleaned out half the medicine cabinet and showed him all the space in the bathroom drawers he could have. He was pleased with even these simple things that made it more real. Proof that he was part of my world and I wanted him there.

And he showed me the start of his business plan with Roman. He sent me photos he'd taken and asked for my opinion on complicated things like composition and lighting. And we talked endlessly about stuff I'd usually find boring, but with Sasha it was anything but.

Connor wouldn't believe my shift in interest to all things business. I always left that stuff to him, preferring to do something with my hands and leave the office work to him. Since I brought internet to the lodge and now see how easy it is to do my books with a program, I often apologize to Connor while doing it.

He always had great ideas, but I admit, I was stubborn most times and never listened. Connor was a gem that way, always putting up with my old school attitude.

I still miss him, but it's different now. I can't put words to it, but I smile more when I think of him. Connor would like to know I still laugh and smile at him, even though he's not here. It's been a long road for me to get to a place where his memory brings me more joy than sadness. There're still sad days, but I roll with them as they come and I don't let the grief swamp me when it shows up.

Making sure I have my keys, wallet and phone, I take the stairs down to the kitchen.

And stop dead in my tracks at the sight before me.

"Leaf! What do you think? He'll like it, right?"

Millie beams at me over the table covered in maple creme filled cookies, Sasha's guilty pleasure that she's sent to him three times already.

"That's a lot of cookies. It will take him months to eat those."

"Well, they aren't all for him. Go look out in the dining room."

I don't know what she's getting at, but I go to the dining room and again, I'm speechless.

"What do you think? Is this too much?" Pete asks from on top of the ladder where he's hanging tiny lights in the shape of stars.

"Uh... too much for what, exactly?"

"For Sasha. To welcome him and for you two to have a housewarming party."

Baffled, I shake my head. "But I already live here."

Perry sets a box of decorations down next to me.

"You didn't read those romance books at all, did you?" He shakes his head, the disappointment clear.

"Well, not like cover to cover."

"Just the sexy bits, then?"

"I...well..." Rubbing my neck, I shoot him a glare. "Maybe."

Some of those books are very descriptive. I'm just a man. Alone. With a renewed sex drive. Sue me for appreciating word porn. I learned that term at the bookstore when I was eavesdropping and it's very appropriate.

"Your man loves romance. I've been trying to tell you, but you don't listen."

He holds up a roll of white gauzy stuff to Pete. "Is the tulle too much? Do you think it will add to the romance or is it too 1980s wedding vibe?"

Tulle? What the fuck is tulle?

"Oh! Good idea! I think we can use it on that topiary thing."

Topiary?

"So you guys have a welcome party for him? And you're making it romantic?"

"We're making it with things he loves." Perry raises his eyebrow. "Because we read the books he likes. Catch up, brother."

"Well, thank you? I think? I was just going to meet him at the airport and bring him home."

Even saying he's coming home sets loose a battalion of butterflies in my gut. He'll be here. Permanently.

"Ahh, I love it when you smile like that when only his name is mentioned. It's good on you." Perry climbs down from his ladder and claps me on the shoulder. "But you're not just gonna meet him, right?"

They both look at me, expectant smiles on their faces, and I feel like I'm a contestant on a game show.

"Nooo... I'm... stopping at the florist? Yeah."

"Oh great! And what are you going to get?"

Perry rubs his hands together with far too much enthusiasm.

"Carnations?"

They both frown, so I hurry to correct myself. "Roses?"

"Classic romance." Perry sighs. "What colour?"

"Ok, listen, I was going to ask the florist to make something for me while I stood there. That's the truth."

"Well, that's good. They'll know best. I think it's roses, though."

Pete nods in agreement and I wonder if I stepped into another dimension where my brother and father figure have suddenly acquired a taste for all things romance and flowers.

Shaking my head, I walk back to the kitchen, where Millie meets me with a smile.

"What do you think?"

"I think you've all lost your minds. But also, thank you. He'll love it."

"You're okay with it, right? When I brought it up last week, you seemed okay with it."

"You asked if I wanted a welcome home party?"

"No, I asked if we could do something to make Sasha feel welcome. It grew to a party. Not that the guest list is that large, but... I didn't think it would be an issue."

"It's not. I'm moved. You're all so excited to have him here." Leaning down, I kiss her cheek. "He'll love it, and I should've put more thought into something like this. I've just been...I don't know, too excited reorganizing my closet to think of this."

We both laugh and she squeezes my hands. We don't need to say the words. She's been a part of my life since I first met Connor, and she's never left. We've celebrated and grieved together and all things in between.

From late night crying sessions in the kitchen to finding me chopping wood at 3 A.M. while screaming, Millie walked with me through it all. Having her approval and support for Sasha means the world to me.

"Happy is good on you, Leaf. I'm so pleased you found it again. Now take a few cookies with you for that man and get on the road."

She pops a few into a bag and hands them to me.

"Thanks Millie. I'll see you in a few hours."

I rush out the front with a wave to Pete and Perry. Once in my truck, I plug in my phone to charge, but before driving off, I send a text to Sasha.

Standing in the arrivals area, I clutch the enormous bouquet in front of me. The arrivals board finally updates his flight to '*Arrived*' and I rush to the doors where weary passengers stream through.

The moment he breaks through the door and sees me, the entire world knows.

"Leaf!"

Sasha barrels towards me, barely missing knocking a woman down. I drop the flowers to the floor when he throws himself at me, wrapping his arms around my neck. My instant reaction is to wrap my arms around his waist and spin him around. Which I do while he peppers my face with kisses.

"I'm here. You're here. I'm so fucking happy to see you."

Setting him down, I look for the flowers and a kind man off to the side holds them for us.

"I didn't want the crowd to trample them." He passes them back to me with a smile. "It's nice to see two people so in love. You have a wonderful day."

I thank him and present them to Sasha. The florist asked me for his favourite colours and a little about us. Pink and purple I know Sasha loves, along with black and various shades of green.

The florist put together a mixed bouquet of pink and white roses—Perry will be thrilled—-and added tiny little purple flower things. It's very pretty, and he assured me Sasha would love it.

"You did this for me?" He brings the flowers to his nose and inhales. A soft smile on his lips as he gently touches a rose petal.

"Yeah. Do you like them?"

"No one has ever got me flowers before." His voice hitches, but I lift his chin with a finger. Beautiful brown eyes stare back at me and now I understand what the guys meant about romance. He always looks at me in a way that makes me feel like I'm a marshmallow swimming in a mug of hot chocolate, but right now I feel like a god who created the world.

"Beauty, I will give you the world if I can. This is just the beginning."

His lip trembles, but he doesn't cry. No, my Sasha is strong. Not that tears would be inappropriate or weak, but it's no longer his instant response to my words or gestures. Instead, he smirks before kissing me so soundly I'm left breathless.

With the flowers now smashed between us and the arrivals area almost empty, he whispers against my lips.

"And what a beginning it is. Take me home so we can get started."

"I like the sounds of that."

Tugging me by the hand towards the luggage pickup, he throws me that magazine worthy smile over his shoulder, and I just about break into a dance.

Sasha was so overwhelmed with the little party at the lodge when he arrived, he could barely speak to thank everyone. Like the social butterfly he is, I watched from the side as he hugged everyone he met the first time he was here and had private conversations with each of them.

Especially Perry.

All the tiny lights that looked like stars left him amazed. The cookies, of course, he was thrilled with, but it was the simple gesture from my brother that left him struggling for words.

"I still can't believe Perry did that for me. We got off on the wrong foot several times and he's really a nice guy."

Sasha sits next to me on the sofa, shower fresh and smelling like coconut. He snuggles up next to me, pulling the quilt off the back of the couch to cover his legs.

"To be fair, I think he's a closet romantic. He bought you the gift card for the bookstore with ulterior motives. He wants to read what you pick. I guarantee it."

"Well, don't make it sound like he wasn't being thoughtful!" He smacks my leg playfully. "He also gave me the reading journal that was monogrammed. It was lovely."

"I know. You had a hard time speaking. He does like you, though, and he's happy to have you back here. We all are."

Sasha squirms around to face me and places his hand on my cheek.

"I was going to wait, but there's something I've been thinking about a lot. I'd like to show you if I could?"

He scans my face, and he's so sincere and hopeful. He curls his fingers into my short beard and I hum. I love it when he does that.

"This sounds serious. You sure?"

"Yes. I... it's been on my mind since before I left here in the summer."

"Okay. You can show me."

After placing a soft kiss on my cheek, he retrieves his laptop bag from the living room and pulls out an orange plastic Duotang. He puffs out a breath and turns back to me. His knee bounces just enough that the Duotang jiggles in his hands.

"You've talked about Connor a lot. You've shared with me how you met and who he was, not just to you, but to this whole town." He swallows and stares at his lap. "When you took me on the trails at your sugar shack, I noticed the change in you. You had this great longing in your voice I hadn't heard before. And you told me it was that piece of property that brought you here. It brought Connor to you."

He removes the blank page from the folder's front cover and flips it over. Recognizing the cabin and my processing building, I sit up straighter. He finally turns to me and holds out the Duotang.

"This is a business plan. I made it with Roman's help and some research on the maple syrup industry. So it could very well be inaccurate. But... the first two parts are what I'd really like to do for you." He swallows. "And Connor."

Flipping open the cover, the title page blazes at me in bright orange, just like the Duotang.

Connor's Cabin

Quickly scanning the multi-page document, my breathing picks up and the pages blur. His soft hands wipe the wetness from my cheeks without a word as I try to process the words I'm reading.

"You want to renovate my cabin and restart my maple syrup production?" I finally meet his soft gaze. "And name it after Connor?"

"Yes."

"Why?"

He caresses my cheek, his thumb still wiping at the stray tears I can't contain.

"Because without him, there's no you. And without you, there's no me. In a twisted way, Connor brought us together, and he means everything to you. Just because he's gone doesn't mean he's forgotten. And I want you to know that it never makes me uncomfortable for you to talk about him."

Never did I think I'd fall in love the first time it happened. Connor was so persistent and he was just easy to love. Maybe that's what made his death so hard. Because it wasn't easy accepting my love was gone forever. I have seven years of proof.

Now I have Sasha. A second love. Another chance to share my heart with someone. And he doesn't want me to forget my first love.

"My mom left me a trust and I know she would've wanted me to use it for my future. That's you, Leaf. You're my future and I want us to do this together in the same spirit you had when you first dreamed of your own sugar shack. It's important to me that we include Connor somehow."

"I don't know what to say. This is..."

Swallowing hard, I gather him in my arms and hold on tight. He clutches at me just as tight and whispers how grateful he is to have found me.

In the quiet of the night, a single loon calls, the sound drifting to us, even inside.

That's my sign.

And a peace I've not felt in years settles over me.

Epilogue

18 months later
Leaf

"Do you have enough photos yet, Sasha? I'm dying here."

He peers over his camera at me and that look will never fail to make my heart speed up.

"I was done a while ago. I just like looking at you through the camera and imagining you naked."

Walking over to me, he snaps at my suspender with a playful grin.

"I'm going to ask Roman to design something with suspenders and not much else."

"You're a bit rotten, you know."

He laughs as I set the axe down safely and scoop him into my arms.

"You may have mentioned it once or twice."

"Can you believe we're finally here to open this to the public? I'm so excited I'm shaking."

Sasha squeezes my hand tight as we turn to survey all our hard work. Since he presented me the plan for re-starting my sugar shack, we jumped right in. With help from Perry when he was available, the three of us did as much work ourselves as possible before hiring local people to finish. Turns out Sasha isn't half bad with power tools and paintbrushes.

While I thought the cabin here could be used for his studio later with Roman, he had bigger ideas and I'm glad I listened.

"I know it's small, but when you come to the source of the maple syrup, you should be able to have it on pancakes."

My former two-room cabin has been transformed into a self-serve pancake house. We cleared an area next to the cabin and built several picnic tables for people to sit and enjoy what they stuffed into their takeout containers. And of course there's no shortage of maple syrup and other maple products—like Millie's maple crème-filled cookies.

"And it has nothing to do with your addiction to pancakes?"

He bats his eyelashes with a grin. "Not at all. But it's rather convenient."

Together, we cleaned all the tapping lines and spouts, the buckets, and machines. We worked our whole first winter together on this project as much as possible. Once the spring came, I had to be full-time at the lodge and Sasha had to concentrate on finishing his photography course.

Not to mention his own business venture with Roman.

Sasha was someone I wasn't prepared for. Not the first time he arrived here with his designer clothes and uncertainty. And definitely not when he came back to stay with his newfound confidence and sense of self. His determination to make something of himself, and us, never fails to leave me wondering how lucky I am to be the recipient of his affection.

"I love you. If it wasn't for you, none of this would have happened."

"It would have, Leaf. Maybe not like this, but you'd have made your way here, eventually. This is who you are. You just needed a push to get back to life."

He kisses the back of my hand, and I focus on his pink, glossy lips. The same lips I kiss every day and listen to encouraging words from.

"I know that look, Leaf, and we can't."

With a chuckle, I kiss his neck and walk him back to the doorway.

"What look?"

A nibble to his ear and he sighs.

"The one that says you want me naked and spread out in three seconds."

A whisper near his ear so my beard feathers across his cheek and neck. I know he likes that. He sucks in a sharp breath.

"You'd be right. And I know we can't... yet. And the whole time we do this event and the reporters ask questions, just think of what we used to do here before it became a pancake house." I feather a kiss on his neck. "Because I'm doing it as soon as we get home."

He turns his head and takes my lips in a desperate kiss. And I'd lose my control and strip him naked anyway if it weren't for the sounds of tires crunching into the lot.

"Our first guests. You ready for this?"

"I'm ready for anything. Let's do it."

Sasha

The grand opening is far more successful than I imagined. People came out for Leaf by the hundreds on this chilly February day and I don't think it's possible for my heart to be more full for him.

Perry drove the tractor, pulling wagons of people through the bush while Leaf explained the tapping lines and collection process. A few times I joined him on the ride and it was a thrill to see him so animated, talking about something he was a thousand percent into.

Mostly, though, I manned the cash and sold maple syrup by the crapload.

And ate pancakes.

Talk about living a magical life.

The door to our apartment closes behind us and after Leaf drops his keys on the counter, he collapses on the sofa face down.

"That was a long day, beauty."

He turns his head instead of mumbling into the couch cushions.

Tossing my coat over a chair, I kneel over him and massage his shoulders.

"It was indeed. But it was so perfect."

He hisses when I hit a sore spot. "Right there, Sash. Fuck, that hurts, but it's so good."

"Are you up for the party in town later?"

"It's in honour of Connor's Cabin. I have to be there."

I was only playing with names when I suggested Connor's Cabin, but every time he says it, I swell with pride.

"I guess you're right. So the thing you promised earlier? Is that off the table?"

His body shakes with laughter underneath me.

"Normally I don't turn you down, but I don't think I can stay awake at a party if I bend you over the couch right now."

He pushes to sit up, so I move and once he's sitting, I crawl back onto his lap. Leaf is one of those people who says everything with his eyes. His warm brown eyes are always filled with a tender affection for me. It doesn't matter if he's angry at me for leaving a mess on the bathroom counter or a post-sex gaze, I know he loves me more than anyone ever has. Not only more, but in a way that aligns with my soul.

Over the last year and a half, this man has nurtured every part of me. From professional ideas, to how much I make myself a part of the lodge, and intimate moments like these.

Sometimes his intensity stops my heart. Like now.

"I'm really proud of you, Leaf. You had just as big a part in this as I did."

"Thanks. And I know. We're a good team."

He pulls me down for a kiss that's so passionate and spine-tingling I have to break away.

"You said you can't do both. I don't want you missing the party."

His thumb brushes over my kiss-swollen lips, and he swallows. The click of his throat is louder than the short pants of air I call breathing.

"Thank you for everything, Sasha. I have no words to tell you how grateful I am for you in my life, but I know without you there'd be a lot less light."

"Without you, I have nowhere to shine it. You gave me the courage to do that and I'll never forget the first time you made me feel seen, Leaf. You keep doing it, too. Every single time you look at me like you are now." With a gentle kiss to his lips, I stand and offer my hand.

"You have a party to dress for. I'll still be horny when we get back."

Leaf's laughter and smile are the greatest thing.

"I know you will. You picked out suspenders, didn't you?"

"Yep. You can thank me later."

Perry

Fuck, it's great to see my brother happy.

I've missed this sugar shack. Sasha was the answer to my prayers to have my brother return to the land of the living again. I know Leaf grieved the loss of Connor hard. I've never had a spouse, so I don't know what it's like to lose one that way.

But I loved Connor like another brother, and it brought me to my knees when he died. The difference between me and Leaf is that I grieved in private and stayed strong for my brother. Only recently have I even considered giving myself any credit for that.

But with Sasha comes Roman.

The biggest fucking pain in the ass I've ever met.

Lucky me, I get to drive him home tonight after the big party downtown. Leaf and Sasha made their appearances, and the press ate it up. Sasha surprised Leaf with an announcement to plant a new tree in Connor's park downtown and I'm man enough to admit it brought a tear to my eye.

Roman not so much. He's a thorn in my side.

"Are you ready yet?"

The pain in question slams his empty glass on the bar and peers at me with glassy eyes.

"I've been ready for at least thirty minutes. You said you wanted to finish your drink."

He looks at the empty glass, then back to the door of the men's washroom. A man exits with messed up hair and a smile as big as Texas on his face. He nods at Roman and clears his throat before turning in the opposite direction.

"Seriously? In the bathroom? Could you be any more cliché?"

Tossing a tip down for the bartender, I grab my coat and motion toward the door.

"What's that supposed to mean? I had spontaneous sex. It's not cliché. You're a cliché. Do you own anything not plaid?"

He sniffs and strolls to the coat check, leaving me behind.

"I like plaid."

"And I like sex. So we're even."

The girl hands him his coat. It's a giant white puffy thing, and he looks like an oversized marshmallow. I can't hold my laughter in.

"What's so funny?"

"You remind me of a marshmallow in that thing. The big one from *Ghostbusters*."

His response is to stalk away and expect me to follow.

And I do, because my brother asked me to so he could leave early with Sasha. It's nights like this I wish I wasn't single.

The February air still carries some iciness and I wouldn't mind snuggling up with a warm body tonight.

But instead, I need to get a diva back to the lodge and it's too late to call any of my casual hooks-ups. Maybe I should just try to make the best of it with Roman's company.

"Your vehicle is filthy. I'm sending you the dry cleaning bill if my coat gets stained."

And there goes that thought.

There's nothing about Roman's company I want to keep.

The next story is Perry and Roman! Kiss My Axe is coming soon!

Not ready to say goodbye? Get a free short story with Leaf and Sasha, Guitar Strings and Pretty Things.

What's next?

Curious about Sasha's adventures on a mechanical bull? You can read about it in Alec.

If you want to stay in the town of Maple a little longer, check out my contribution to the Truth or Dare Anthology.

Or check out the *also by* page and start at the beginning of the RM-verse. All my books cross over and connect in some way but don't need to be read in order.

Acknowledgements

What a ride, huh? Did you run out of tissues like I did?

Let me first say thank you for reading. This story was more angsty than my usual and it wrung me out. But it was a story that just took on a life of it's own, so I went with it. Thank you for trusting me and reading it through.

When I began writing this, it was supposed to be a light, grumpy sunshine romance. But, as minds and hearts often do, I wandered down a different path. Perhaps fate was preparing me for what was to come. Seven days after I finished the first draft of Beauty and the Beard, my dad passed away. It wasn't unexpected — cancer sucks — but a shock, nonetheless.

So this book is extra special to me. I hope you enjoyed Leaf and Sasha.

As always, I have people to thank.

My brother will never read this, but thank you for holding me up when I was just as broken as you. Without you, I couldn't have got through finding that damn broken loon dish at dad's apartment and taking it home.

Friends, the coincidences in this book and my dad passing away are crazy. The loon dish is only one of them.

Jenn Green, oh gosh, I'm so sorry I made you snot cry editing this. But thank you for the running commentary and understanding where my mind was. You've been more than an editor during all this and I can't thank you enough.

The members of my reader group, Neill's Naughty List. You were there for me when I needed an outlet, and I'm so very grateful to have you all. Not just for your support with all these stories I create, but for your genuine care for my family.

Kota, thank you for listening when I was stuck. That's it, lol. You always know what to say.

Thank you to my friends and fellow authors, Travis Beaudoin and Ava Olsen, who kindly allowed me to reference their books in this story. If you haven't read Too Like the Lightning or The Cockpit, please do. They're two of my favourite reads.

And finally, Janice and Hollie. Teaching you about logging and touring one of Ontario's largest parks sparked my idea of a lumberjack series with all the plaid loving members of a small town. Inspiration is everywhere. Thank you for helping me find this one.

Thank you, dear reader for picking up this book and trusting me. Without you there's no stories to tell.

Until next time,

RM

Also By

Want to read more by me?
Scan the code to find my back list.

www.ingramcontent.com/pod-product-compliance
Lightning Source LLC
Chambersburg PA
CBHW072055190726
48294CB00005B/1540